THE LAST WITCH OF KALHOUN HOLLER

THE LAST WITCH OF KALHOUN HOLLER

MARMALADE AND MAGIC™ BOOK 1

MICHAEL ANDERLE

This book is a work of fiction. All of the characters, organizations, and events portrayed in this novel are either products of the author's imagination or are used fictitiously. Sometimes both.

Copyright © 2022 LMBPN Publishing
Cover by Fantasy Book Design
Cover copyright © LMBPN Publishing
A Michael Anderle Production

LMBPN Publishing supports the right to free expression and the value of copyright. The purpose of copyright is to encourage writers and artists to produce the creative works that enrich our culture.

The distribution of this book without permission is a theft of the author's intellectual property. If you would like permission to use material from the book (other than for review purposes), please contact support@lmbpn.com. Thank you for your support of the author's rights.

LMBPN Publishing
PMB 196, 2540 South Maryland Pkwy
Las Vegas, NV 89109

Version 1.00, April 2022
ebook ISBN: 979-8-88541-450-0
Print ISBN: 979-8-88541-451-7

THE LAST WITCH OF KALHOUN HOLLAR TEAM

Thanks to our Beta Readers

Larry Omans, John Ashmore, Rachel Beckford, Kelly O'Donnell

Thanks to our JIT Readers

Zacc Pelter
Christopher Gilliard
Wendy L Bonell
Diane L. Smith
Dorothy Lloyd
Dave Hicks
Angel LaVey

Editor

Lynne Stiegler

CHAPTER ONE

"Why's it got to be so damn hot here?" Jemma Nox muttered as she peered toward the sun between the pine trees around the house. It glared down, mocking her. She searched the sky, but no signs of rain were visible. She glanced down. The grass all over the property was brown. It had been an unusually dry season.

Summer was at its peak. The August air was as hot and sticky in Kalhoun County, Tennessee as it had been in Jemma's former home in the suburb of Hendricks, Indiana. The sixteen-year-old swiped dark auburn hair out of her sweaty face and sighed. The cool of autumn couldn't come soon enough.

Something about her new home seemed to perpetuate the heat. It just wouldn't end. The summer had been long, hot, and strenuous. In former years, Jemma would have been more than happy to have summer last forever, but this year was different. She had two years of high school left, and she wanted nothing more than to leave this simmering summer behind and get on with her life.

New beginnings were ahead, and she didn't want to think about her past life anymore. She was tired of everything that had happened before. So damn tired.

"I need a nap," she grumbled as she trudged up the front porch steps of her new home. Though they had begun the moving process a week ago, they had made little progress on unpacking since their arrival. She walked in and had to maneuver around piles of unopened boxes. She frowned. Her father hadn't done a very good job of marking the boxes. She had no way in hell of telling which box held which items, and ones marked Fragile were overturned or set precariously on top of other boxes.

Jemma sighed, wishing for the nap she'd been thinking about all morning. She made her way around the box obstacles into the tiny kitchen, which was combined with an even smaller dining room. Her father sat at the round table. For some reason, he had unpacked a red and white checkered tablecloth but little else.

Jemma shook her head but couldn't help smiling. Her father, hearing her soft footsteps on the wooden floorboards, looked up. She leaned against the doorframe between the kitchen and the living room, arms crossed. She was tall like her father and had similarly shaped features. Her auburn hair and light brown eyes, however, had been inherited from her mother.

Thaddeus Nox went by the nickname "Tad." It was so normal among his family and friends that even his daughter used it rather than "Dad." He looked up, his dark eyes meeting Jemma's. His brown hair had grown almost to his shoulders, and his new beard was streaked with gray.

He hadn't had long hair or a beard the entire time he was married to Jemma's mother, but he was trying "a new look.

Jemma tried to suppress her thoughts about this new Tad since one of her greatest weaknesses was her inability to keep her feelings from showing on her face. He looked like a mountain man, which, she decided, made sense, given their new surroundings.

"Hey there, Jem. Look at this." His voice was cheery as he beckoned her in. Jemma liked being with her father when he was cheerful. It was a good change after the years of depression he had endured as she watched helplessly. He scooted a stool over for her to sit on. Jemma didn't know where it had come from, but she sat on it and leaned forward. Her father extended a pamphlet.

Jemma sighed. "I'd rather not talk about school for another two weeks." She leaned back. The pamphlet read Solomon's Cross High. That was the institution her father wanted her to begin attending in two weeks when the fall semester started. "I wanted to be homeschooled for the rest of high school. You know that."

The thought of starting over had been a relief to Jemma at first, but the whole "making new friends at a new school thing" wasn't at the top of her list of desirable new experiences.

"My whole life was in Hendricks," she complained as if she'd had a former life in the suburb outside of Indianapolis to lament. She'd had few friends, and they had been around more for the sake of convenience than anything else. She doubted any of them would keep in touch with her for longer than a month.

"I know, sweetheart, but you'll become a hermit like

your old man, doin' that," Tad told her with a kind smile. He squeezed her shoulder.

Jemma shrugged. "I can make friends. I just don't want to make them at school."

Tad chuckled and shook his head. "Try it, Jem. For me? Just try."

Jemma couldn't help but grin and give in. Her father used the same words she had used when trying to convince him to move out of Hendricks. "Try it, Dad. For me? Just try." She had said those words day after day until, at last, he had agreed to move.

"Where to, Jem?" he had asked her.

"Anywhere you want. Anywhere you think will make you better," she had replied.

Tad Nox had chosen to move them to Kalhoun County, Tennessee, to a small one-bedroom house with a loft nestled in the Appalachian Mountains. It wouldn't be so bad, Jemma thought. Anywhere was better than the small suburban town where running into her mom was a possibility at any given time. Here, she could go to a grocery store or the movie theater without having to worry about seeing the one person who stirred up a confounding amount of resentment and anger within her.

The image of Delilah Nox's face flashed across her mind. She pushed the thought of her mother aside for the time being. She had more important things to face. "What're we having for dinner, Tad?" She stood and began rifling through the boxes piled in the kitchen.

For the past several weeks, the two of them had lived on takeout, delivered pizza, untoasted Pop Tarts, and cereal without milk. Jemma was ready for a home-cooked meal. It didn't seem like that would be possible tonight. None of the dishes had been unpacked. The boxes containing them weren't even in the kitchen.

"You've got your 'annoyed with Dad's packing skills' face on again," Tad remarked with a chuckle.

Jemma gestured at a box while trying to smile. "I don't understand why the oven mitts are in the same box as your tools and your socks and the TV remotes? Where is the TV?"

Tad shifted, his eyes drifting about the kitchen and into the darkened living room. "I've been wondering the same thing. I have a game I want to watch."

Jemma glowered, which made Tad laugh more. She continued to search the boxes. Now that the task was begun, she didn't see an end in sight. The thought of food was driven clean out of her mind. She wanted to sleep on a bed tonight with sheets and pillowcases, dammit. What she did not find in the next box, however, was sheets or pillowcases.

She frowned. "What's all this shit?"

"Jem—" her father started.

Before he could rebuke her language, Jemma added, "Really, Dad? Why?" She pulled out a pile of faded papers, pictures, and small miscellaneous items. There was a plethora of things: printed photographs, handwritten letters, ticket stubs, and more. There was even a perfume sample of the scent her mother always wore.

Jemma's suspicions about the items were confirmed when she found the last of the collection: a ring box. She doubted it was empty. The glittering diamond wedding ring had long since left her mother's finger and been returned to the box. Her father was still holding onto things from his failed marriage, and that was the last thing he needed to be doing.

Jemma gave him a reproachful look. Tad stood up, looking sheepish. He scratched his head and plunged his hands deep into his pockets. He opened his mouth to give some excuse, but Jemma didn't let him. "You promised a fresh start. You promised me you wouldn't bring these things."

There was a hint of sorrow in her father's expression. It wasn't until she saw the conflicting emotions in his eyes that Jemma realized her posture had stiffened and her face revealed her disappointment. She softened her features. Her father didn't deserve any more admonishment than he had been given in the past two years.

The proximity of her mother in Hendricks, Indiana had done Tad more harm than it had Jemma. Not only had her mother chosen to abandon them for a "better life," but she hadn't even had the decency to move away. She had stayed in town, the very town she had grown up in where the people were *her* people, not Tad's. Tad gradually became a stranger to the people he had once called close friends.

On several occasions, Jemma had come home from school to find her father sitting in a dim living room, nursing a bottle of liquor or a cigarette. Whenever this happened, Jemma knew he had seen her. He had seen his ex-wife Delilah Nox in a grocery store or at a gas station and been reminded of the joy and pain he had experienced during their twenty-year relationship. Jemma was determined not to allow to her father to succumb to any form of addiction. They had to get away.

So here they were in Tennessee, and she still wasn't sure what had drawn her father to this place. She didn't know why he had chosen to move here.

"I'm sorry, Jem. I broke my promise to you," Tad replied. He did look remorseful.

I need to throw the damn things away and be done with it, Jemma thought, but then pity for her father overwhelmed the anger stirring within her—the anger that bade her get rid of any sign of Delilah having ever been a part of their lives. What followed her pity was a pang of guilt at the thought of throwing away her father's property without his permission, even if the property was doing a damn good job of poisoning him emotionally.

Tad gave her a wan smile. "I'll look up what's in town, and we'll find somewhere to go eat."

Conversation over, he left the room. Jemma waited until his footsteps faded into his bedroom before she crept up to the loft with the items from his marriage in hand. A mattress sat on the floor amid boxes she hoped held all of her belongings. To her left, at the top of the ladder, was a closet. She opened it and was greeted by a billow of dust. She coughed and waved her hand until it cleared. Jemma peered in. Cobwebs lined the corners. The space didn't look like it had been used in a very long time.

Jemma bent down and wrangled things around. She moved boxes she had tossed in the day before without opening them. Her goal now was to hide her father's belongings in the corner and cover them with her clothes. When she pushed farther into the closet, she thumped against its back. She cried out in alarm as the panel came down upon her.

"That fucking hurt!" she hissed, hoping her father hadn't heard the ruckus from his room below. She paused and listened. No reaction came. She stood up, moving the panel off her as she straightened. Now she was both sweaty from being outside and dusty from the closet. Further, the loft was suffocatingly hot since they hadn't been able to get the air conditioning working yet.

All of those things fell away, however, when Jemma realized where the panel had come from. There was a false back to the closet. Whoever had used it last hadn't put the panel back on properly, and it had shifted at her first contact with it. The real back of the closet was shallow and full of dust and cobwebs, just like the front, but Jemma bent down. There was something in the new space.

Her fingers traced the outline of a small old chest. It just fit in her hands. The outside was covered in dust, and it looked as old as the ancient trees outside. A feeling of intrigue filled Jemma. She had a feeling she wasn't supposed to have this box in her hands, but she opened it anyway.

Faded black and white photographs covered the bottom of the chest. The subjects of the photos were an extended family gathered together at the edge of a wooded area in clothing that looked at least a century out of style. There was also a tattered leather book.

Jemma blew the dust off it. There was a name imprinted on the bottom corner, but it was so faded that she couldn't read it. She opened the volume to find loose scraps of paper filled with writing in a thin, cramped script. She frowned. The light was bad, but she knew that even if she sat in front of the window, she wouldn't be able to make out what was written. Whoever this had belonged to was long gone from this house and probably thought they had lost it.

She examined the words once more, which were written in a spidery scrawl. The hand looked hurried. Jemma couldn't help but be curious. She was more of a science nerd than a history geek, but the idea that what lay before her was the hidden memoir of someone who lived in this particular corner of the United States compelled Jemma to a greater curiosity than she would have believed.

Jemma heard rustling below, followed by her father's cheery voice. "Found a place in town, Jem. There are only two." He chuckled. "I'm ready to go when you are."

Jemma peered over the edge of the loft. "Soon," she replied and turned back to the newfound objects in her hands. A panicked rush of conflicting emotions filled her. She had no clue why.

Why don't I want Dad to see me right now? she wondered. For some reason, all her instincts told her she should keep this to herself. Without thinking about it, Jemma shoved her father's divorce contraband into the closet with her foot and placed the ancient box on top. She kept the photo album in her hand. She didn't want to keep the whole thing from Tad. This was the first interesting thing she'd encountered since they'd arrived, and she wanted to share it.

Tad met her at the ladder. He had climbed up while she was hiding things in the closet. "You good up here, Jem?"

She turned to find his eyes smiling and his lips parted. She nodded. "All good." Instinctively, she closed the closet door and stood in front of it. She didn't want to tell him about the false back, either. She didn't want to lie to her father, but she also didn't want him to see where she had stashed his box of marriage mementos.

Tad seemed to notice none of these things. He did, however, see the photo album in his daughter's hands. "What's that?"

She extended it to him. "I found it up here. It isn't ours."

Tad opened it and glanced at the photographs. He squinted at them through his round glasses. "Very cool, Jem. Very cool," he murmured as he traced his fingers over the images. He shrugged. "Maybe we can find out who this belongs to when we go to town."

Jemma nodded, then tilted her head and observed her father for a long moment. "I think it belonged to whoever lived here last. I wonder why they didn't take it with them?" She also wondered why it had been left hidden behind a false back in the closet. Whoever had stashed it hadn't wanted anyone to find it.

Tad scratched his head. "I bought this home a few months ago, as you know, but I never told you how much of a mystery it was."

He had Jemma's interest. "What do you mean?"

Tad sighed. "The real estate broker told me this house had been sitting empty for some time but had been kept from falling into disrepair by a handyman who had a long contract with someone to keep the place 'in good order.'"

Jemma's brows knitted. "Contracted by who?"

Tad shrugged. "Beyond me. He told us we had the option to keep the handyman if we wanted. I haven't decided. I haven't even met the man."

"Who owned it before us?" Jemma asked.

"A woman named Mabel Doire, I believe, was the name he gave me." Tad looked down at the photo album. "I wonder if this Ms. Doire is one of the women in the photographs?" He glanced at his daughter. "We'll bring this along to dinner." He went back down the ladder. Jemma followed, not wanting the photo album to leave her sight. She couldn't put her finger on why. Possessiveness toward it overcame her.

"I'm ravenous!" Tad exclaimed, grinning as he exited their house. They got into his truck and made their way into town, the closest thing in the area of Solomon's Cross to a downtown center.

Jemma glanced in the rearview mirror as they pulled out of the gravel driveway. The woods on the left of the property struck her as familiar. As their home disappeared in the distance, she realized why. The photographs of the people in the album had been taken in front of those trees.

CHAPTER TWO

Solomon's Cross in the Eastern Tennessee Appalachian Mountains was an area whose days of coal boom had never really come. Despite that, the town had not withered like so many other small towns around it.

The sun was beginning to set when the blue truck carrying Tad Nox and his daughter rattled into town. The sky bled scarlet beyond the old buildings flanking the narrow, dusty street. Driving down the main thoroughfare of Solomon's Cross felt like slipping into the past. Jemma peered out the window with her brows drawn together. Everything here looked tired, like it needed the nap she had never gotten that day.

Jemma thought back to why her father had chosen to come here. Or rather, to the reason he had given to her. Tad had been hired by a telecom company to assure the quality of new fiber optic cable soon to be run around the mountains, which would make Solomon's Cross a convenient central hub for various locations Tad was responsible for.

Jemma's eyes moved from the buildings, trucks, people, and the road up to the pine-tree-lined mountains. The huge rocks snuggled close, holding everything in the town below them in tight proximity. Even though there were dozens of roads coming in and out of the mountains, Jemma felt closed in when she looked at her surroundings.

She was glad to have left Hendricks, but she wasn't happy about where they had ended up. Out the window to her right loitered a group of teenage boys about her age. They looked like the same kind of bad news she had known at her old school. They were restless young men who were looking for a good time despite what it cost another person.

She thought about the new school her father wanted her to go to, but she shoved the thoughts away and took her eyes off the boys. They leaned against the glass of a storefront, smoking, not bothered by anyone seeing them.

The truck rattled to a stop in front of their destination. Harv's Hamburgers & Hotcakes was as "small town diner" as you could get. Jemma stepped out of the truck and wrinkled her nose. The smell of smoke hung heavy in the air. She shut the passenger side door with more force than she'd intended, drawing a surprised look from her father. She ignored him and stepped to the diner's door. When it opened, a bell rang, signaling the patrons inside to a new arrival.

If what Jemma had already seen of the area wasn't enough to convince her of its very small-town nature, what happened next wouldn't allow her to deny it. Every pair of eyes slid toward the newcomers. Upon not seeing familiar faces, the eyes narrowed and seemed to stick. The looks ranged from interest to bemusement to outright hostility. Jemma's eyes met those of a ten-year-old boy, a middle-aged trucker, and then an old woman with a shrewd glance and a pinched expression before she quit trying to make eye contact. Different expressions were scattered across the diner's patrons like pancake batter.

Why the hell do they have to look at us like that? Jemma thought as her eyes sought an empty booth. All the stools at the counter were occupied. Behind her was a corkboard with a display of photos and clippings about local events and heroes. Stepping forward, she realized that the smoke she smelled had yellowed and curled the photos and clippings stuck there.

The items on the board had been there for a long time, it seemed. The information on many of them dated back to World War II. The torn newspaper articles and scribbles on the photographs revealed the old men like gnarled trees who had planted their asses in their traditional seats decades ago.

Jemma frowned. If any of the people in this town were like what she assumed all these men in the pictures were, she wasn't going to like it here very much. "Narrow-minded Midwesterners or some shit," she muttered. "No different from Indiana." No one seemed to hear her, and that was probably for the best.

Jemma's attention was drawn away by her father's voice. "Empty booth right over there." He pointed, and they went over together. The bright red upholstery on the booth's seats was torn and peeling. When Jemma sat down, she sank in and fought back a groan. Was this the best place in town? If so, she had better get used to it. At this point, she wasn't sure about their move here. Couldn't they have gone to another town that was better, or were they all like this?

She glanced at the food on the plates on the table next to them. The selection looked like it would taste fantastic until five minutes after the last bite. Then, Jemma would realize that death by diabetes or heart disease would feel like it was only moments away. *Or both diabetes* and *heart disease,* she thought, trying not to grumble out loud. *Wouldn't that be a combination?*

Eyes remained on the pair even as they sat down. Jemma fought the desperate urge to cringe. Tad chuckled and waved at the onlookers. Jemma rolled her eyes. Her father was her opposite; He could make friends anywhere he went. Tad Nox knew no strangers. Jemma, however, felt like a stranger everywhere she went, with anyone she was with. Anyone but her father. She even held her friends back home at an arm's length. That was just as well, now that she was gone from them and would not be returning anytime soon.

After Tad's friendly wave and smile, the eyes broke free of the pair one by one. Conversations that had stopped when they came in resumed like a phonograph finding the right groove again after an unexpected bump.

After they were seated, a stout woman in an apron wobbled over to them. Strings of loose gray hair hung on either side of her pudgy face. Jemma realized that here was a no-nonsense kind of lady, though not unfriendly. "My name's Barb. I'll be your server," she murmured as if this job at the diner was the last place she wanted to be. She set down napkins and silverware before pouring Tad a cup of coffee.

"Uh, oh…no thanks, ma'am," Tad stammered.

The waitress paused with raised brows.

"Don't particularly like coffee, that's all," Tag added with a friendly smile.

Barb gave him a questioning look before shrugging and taking out a pad and a pen. "What'll it be, then?"

Tad and Jemma gave her their drink orders. The waitress held her pen poised over the pad but didn't write. She gave them bored nods before handing over two dingy menus. Jemma took one look at them and decided the menu hadn't been updated since 1970, except for perhaps some lamination in 1980. She turned to the back of the menu and noticed the addendums written with an ink pen. Twenty or so years later, the ink was beginning to fade.

Jemma sighed. Her stomach was going to hate her later for what she was about to put in it. She was starving, though, and getting a good idea of what was served in town would help her step into her new life. Their drinks arrived, and Barb stood ready to take their orders. "A minute or two, please?" Tad asked.

Barb frowned as if he had made a ridiculous request, then sighed and moved to the next table where a pair that had come in after them was ready to order.

"We'll be coming here a lot, won't we?" Jemma grumbled as she sank back against the booth. She hadn't realized she'd said the words aloud until her father looked at her over his menu.

"Might be, Jem, unless we take turns cooking at home." He gave her a tired smile. Neither of them was much of a cook. Delilah had been the pro in that department. The past couple of years had forced father and daughter to learn to make basic meals.

Jemma sighed, not taking her eyes off the menu that she wasn't reading. She preferred to look at words instead of at the eyes that swiveled in their direction now and then. "Seems like a lot from our old life won't change."

Her tone was despondent, and Tad noted her unhappiness. He set his menu down and looked at his daughter. Sensing that she had his undivided attention, Jemma's eyes flicked up. Her father's brow creased in worry. "It won't be so bad, I think. I'll be working from home most days like I was before, and you'll go to school—"

Jemma looked at her menu again and put up an emotional wall. She had gotten good at that in the past couple of years, just like her father had gotten good at holding onto things that didn't do him any favors.

Tad sighed. "You know, I never said homeschooling was off the table. I just think you should try real school for a bit."

The term "real school" had always bothered her. She could learn at home just as well, couldn't she? *I can do better at home*, she thought. She wanted to do as she had done in Indiana: a combination of community college correspondence and traditional online education. All of that would remain the same. What would be different was her father's regular trips to the hubs and substations in the circle of mountains and other towns around them. With that going on, he would no doubt try to get her involved in some extra-curricular activity, sport, or club.

As Jemma thought about this, her father brought it up.

"Homeschool could work, but I want you to make friends. Maybe something outside of school could help. I don't want you wallowing when I'm not around."

Jemma stiffened and almost snapped at him about the box of self-flagellating memories stowed in her closet. Her father couldn't very well tell her not to wallow without figuring it out for himself. The waitress arrived again, ready to take their order. "You first," Jemma told her father. She hadn't even begun to decide what she wanted to eat.

Jemma barely heard her father order a grilled cheese sandwich, pickle spears, and potato chips before it was her turn. She pointed at the closest thing on the menu. "This, please." She didn't even know what it was. She wasn't sure she cared. The waitress scribbled down their orders, took their menus, and left without a word.

Jemma sought comfort in her soda. Tad wasn't done with their conversation, however. He had seen the spasm of emotion cross his daughter's face. She had always had a hard time keeping her face from revealing her feelings. Delilah had had trouble with that too. Tad looked across the table at his daughter and saw a younger version of his ex-wife. Compassion surged through him. "I can tell you're not happy, Jem. Please tell me why."

Jemma shifted and made herself look at her father's face. His expression was kind and worried. Right now was not the time to reveal her disappointment, she decided, especially since some of the patrons were still letting their eyes stray toward them. She hated not being honest, so she settled for a partial truth. "I don't have the first clue how to find a job here in Kalhoun County, much less in Solomon's Cross, Dad."

The crease in Tad's brow deepened. "You don't have to worry about a job right now. Why don't you look into joining a club or a church group?"

Jemma shook her head, the thought of joining a youth group almost as unappealing as the ripped upholstery she was sitting on and the smell of something burning in the air. Tad Nox's only daughter had never been very social. "If I'm going to be out and about, I might as well be earning money."

It wasn't that Jemma was greedy, just practical. She knew that as she hurtled toward adulthood, the experience and benefits of earning her own money would become more important. Both her parents had been interested in the arts since long before she was born. Why they had stayed in a small town in Indiana as a painter from out of state and a singer who wanted to leave someday was beyond her. Delilah, as far as she knew, wasn't making any progress in music. Her father had given up painting after she left.

That artistic streak wasn't in Jemma—or if it was, the idea of security, especially when it came to money, was a lot more appealing. "I'll start looking soon, Dad. I'm sure a job will get me acquainted with people."

Tad seemed satisfied for the time being, and since Jemma wasn't usually dishonest with him, he trusted she would do what she said she would.

Their food arrived almost too quickly for Jemma's liking. She glowered at it. She had ordered a burger and fries. All of a sudden, she needed a milkshake to go with it. Barb seemed perturbed, though, so she didn't ask if they had those.

"Thank you," Tad told the waitress.

To Jemma's surprise, Barb's dried lips spread into a smile where only a few teeth could be seen. What teeth were left were yellow. Perhaps she smoked cigarettes on her break but stayed inside the diner. It certainly smelled like it. "Let me know if you need anything else," the woman replied before she turned to wait on other customers. Perhaps the waitress had been struck by the realization that she needed good tips and decided to be more friendly.

"Wait, please," Tad called to her.

Jemma cringed. Barb turned back with raised brows. Jemma knew what was about to happen, and it took everything in her not to groan. "Show our kind waitress the photo album you found, Jem. Go on. Show her." Tad looked like an eager child.

Jemma hesitated, then produced the photo album. Barb seemed uninterested, but that didn't stop Tad from prattling about it. "My daughter here found it in the house we've moved into. We're wondering if anyone in this town knows the people in the photos. Might be the family of the woman who owned the house before us."

"Well, let me have a look, then," Barb responded, still acting as if she wanted to be conversing with anyone but them. Jemma reluctantly handed over her new possession. The waitress flipped through the leather-bound album while Tad continued to speak. Whatever he said was drowned out by the rest of the noise in the restaurant. Eyes had turned to them as his eagerness blasted through Barb's half-hearted resistance.

Jemma watched the waitress' face as it changed. Her disinterest and faked politeness began to shift to earnest curiosity. Her brows furrowed, and a look of recognition crossed her face. Her eyes widened.

She knows who she's looking at, Jemma realized. Perhaps bringing the photo album into this dingy hut they called a diner hadn't been such a bad idea.

Barb turned and beckoned to another waitress, a younger woman with too much bright red lipstick on. "Holly, honey, come take a look here at this. Would you believe it?" Barb shook her head. Holly sauntered over, looking bored until she looked at what Barb's attention was on.

"Well, fuck," she muttered.

"Go get Harv," Barb instructed the young girl. A moment later, a large man bustled out of the kitchen. Jemma assumed it was Harvey, the owner of the diner, but she found out that he was Harvey Jr. His father, who wasn't there at the moment, was the owner. One by one, more people surrounded them. They all seemed to know one another, and they all seemed to understand the importance of what Barb was holding in her hands. Once again, Jemma felt like a stranger. The attention they were paying her and her father made her skin crawl. She began to feel claustrophobic. There were so many damn people around her.

All I wanted was a decent dinner, she complained inwardly. She cast her father a pleading expression. She had to get the hell out of here, but Tad's eagerness and curiosity kept his eyes rooted to the photo album in their waitress' hands.

The people who'd come over, old and young, men and women alike, gave exclamations of amazement. *If I'm going to be stuck here, tell me what the hell is going on!* Jemma wanted to scream. This didn't seem like the time or place, no matter how much she wanted to burst. What did they all know that she didn't?

"Well, we sure do recognize people in this here album. The thing's purty old, ain't it?" remarked Harvey Jr.

Everyone else agreed. There were nods and murmurs of assent. At last, Barb let Tad and Jemma in on the secret. She pointed at one of the figures in a photo. It was a stern, mature, handsome woman standing tall and straight between two other women. Other photos around it showed the same woman among a gaggle of what were probably her children and grandchildren. "This here is Mrs. Eloise Brickellwood," Barb explained.

Jemma didn't see the importance of the name, but all the people around her shifted as if the very name being spoken aloud had caused new energy to surge through the place. At last, Jemma began to notice some things. The patrons around her qualified as senior citizens or were within a decade of same, but none of them could seem to remember a time when the woman in the photograph wasn't a wizened old mama, gray and bent, unlike the image in the book.

"This is her face, that's for certain," Barb remarked. "But her back's too straight here. Too much light in her eyes. None of us ever seen an Eloise that looks like this."

"Yeah, I've never seen her lookin' so young," a balding old man commented. "Even when I was a boy, I remember seein' her shufflin' 'cross the porch of Gran's Rest up that damn mountain, lookin' all ancient."

"And terrifying," Holly added with a shudder. "Been seein' her since I was young, too."

Now, that was interesting. How was it that Holly, a young woman, and a man more than twice her age had seen the same old woman when they were children? They had been born decades apart.

I must have food poisoning and be hallucinating, Jemma thought.

"Terrifying as the hills themselves," Barb murmured, talking to herself and the photograph rather than the people around her.

A shudder passed through Jemma at her words. Why did they affect her so much? What did the waitress mean? Jemma couldn't help herself. "Why would you all be so scared of an old lady?"

The people around her and Tad straightened. Barb snapped the photo album shut and set it on the table with a *thump*, making the cups and silverware rattle on the metal surface. That startled Jemma. The people, who had been pressing too close for her comfort a moment before, drifted off one by one. Only a few remained, including Barb and Harvey Jr.

"What are you two folks doin' round these parts anyhow?" Barb demanded. She crossed her arms. "Sure, some people pass through, like truckers and such, but you say that you've moved in. Why move here?"

Why the hell not? Jemma wanted to retort. A warning look from her father held her back, however.

Tad stammered something incoherent and the waitress sighed, her features softening. "I didn't mean to seem rude. Pardon me. And I mean no disrespect. None of us do." She gestured at those who had drifted off. Eyes were still directed at the scene of interest.

"And we mean no disrespect to Mrs. Brickellwood either." The way Barb said that made Jemma think she was speaking for the sake of the other patrons in the diner, not to her and her father. "The old lady is well-regarded, you see."

Jemma and Tad gave their waitress identical quizzical looks.

Barb gave them a tired smile. "Well, it's just old fools mutterin' about things they can hardly remember. Don't pay nobody any mind if they have anythin' strange to say about the old woman."

This statement, as vague and mysterious as it was, spurred Jemma's curiosity. Barb moved off and refilled the drinks two tables down. Jemma leaned close to her father and lowered her voice. "Is it just me, or are they all acting odd?"

Tad stared at his now-cold food, then began to eat without answering her question. At last, he lifted his head and nodded. "They are odd, yes, but most small communities have their fair share of secrets, rumors, and scandals, Jem. I imagine that such a formidable woman," he pointed at the closed album in which Mrs. Brickellwood was pictured, "with a family as large as she seemed to have, is liable to have created no small stir at one time or another."

He shrugged. "I don't expect any of it amounts to much, but the reality is that in a small town like this, that's to be expected." He shrugged again and shoveled half his grilled cheese sandwich into his mouth at once. "They've got nothing better to do." His last words were muffled as he chewed.

Jemma glanced at her food, unconvinced by her father's

explanation. The comments from the older man and the younger woman about seeing the old woman when they were children decades apart still perplexed her. She had come to a diner wanting to leave with a full stomach. Now, it seemed she would be leaving with more questions about the town they had come to live in.

It wouldn't matter anyway. In the grand scheme of things, the whole ordeal would mean very little. What were the odds that some ancient lady would have a big impact on her life in Solomon's Cross?

Barb passed their table again. "Any pie tonight, folks? We have apple and cherry."

For the first time, Jemma dredged up a smile. "Pie would be great."

Anything to distract her from today's strange events.

CHAPTER THREE

Jemma didn't think much about the photo album during the next week. She wanted to get her feet under her in her new home. She spent the next couple of days unpacking and organizing everything, which proved a difficult feat. They had working air conditioning and a water heater the next day, much to her relief. She didn't have to take cold showers after unpacking all day.

It was still blistering hot outside when the first day of September rolled around and she began school. Her father had consented to let her homeschool if she was able to find a job in the meantime. Jemma was relieved, but finding a job in their new area had proven to be more difficult than she had imagined.

It wasn't only that Kalhoun County was far from a booming metropolis, but everywhere Jemma looked had one reason or another to not hire her. This quickly became both frustrating and perplexing. Each place had a new little hitch to keep her from being considered. She wasn't old enough for Loretta's General Store because they sold alcohol. She wasn't trained enough for Hollenbatch Seniors' Home, which required basic nursing knowledge. The hours at Pinebridge Motel were too weird since they required a cleaner to be available at both checkouts, noon and midnight. Who on earth checked out at midnight, especially at a motel in the middle of the mountains?

Other places simply wanted to hire people they knew better. "When did y'all move in?" was the common question asked even before she could even fill out an application. The question was followed by raised brows and narrowed eyes. The expressions told Jemma she should give up and move on. The sixteen-year-old determined that this new home of hers was bound and determined not to welcome her.

She stood in the middle of the crowded living room among the remaining boxes. Huffing with irritation, she blew a strand of hair out of her face and stood with her hands braced on her hips. With a grunt of frustration, she kicked the nearest thing to her foot, which was a chewed-up tennis ball from a dog she'd had growing up. The dog, a Yorkshire terrier she had loved dearly, was another thing her mother had taken with her.

A week after her first visit to the town's main diner, Jemma had nothing to show other than her general knowledge of the layout in Solomon's Cross since she had spent a lot of time trotting about when she wasn't unpacking. Eyes had met hers, but she hadn't bothered to make any new acquaintances. Meeting people at potential job locations had been tiring enough.

Tad had suggested she ask at Harv's diner to see if they would hire her, but the last place Jemma wanted to work was where the scent of unwashed truckers mingled with burned meat and cigarette smoke. *No, thank you, I'll find anything else,* she thought. She was running out of options, though. If she didn't find a job soon, her father would insist she attend Solomon's Cross High so she could mingle with people in her age group.

Jemma wasn't sure which she wanted less: to be a waitress in a dingy diner and make bad tips because people didn't know her or go to high school where no one would talk to her because they didn't know her.

Jemma observed the chewed-up tennis ball for a second as these thoughts passed through her mind. She picked it up and tossed it into the trash. It was one more thing from her past life she didn't need. Despite all the lows she'd experienced in the Tennessee mountains so far, one thing was simmering on the back burner in her mind. The photo album was tucked under her bed, and the other stuff from the box was still in her closet. Jemma glanced around, remembering that her father would not be back for another few hours. She glanced outside. It was still humid and hot, but the trees were beginning to shed their leaves.

She climbed the ladder to the loft, opened the closet, and took out the items. It was either that or keep unpacking, as she had been doing for days. Her homework was done for the day. Jemma opened the box and peered at the loose papers and their crammed script. The papers looked like they had once been bound together in a journal. She squinted and was able to make out dates at the tops of the pages.

She scooted over to a window so she could see them in a better light. For once, the sun was on her side. "Time to transcribe," she muttered. She found a sheet of paper and a pen and began to copy the words she could distinguish. She discovered she had never heard a lot of the terms before. One of the pages described some type of farming machinery, and another described a car. It was very dull until Jemma began to see the words "the Enemy" scattered about the text.

She scribbled down some things she could safely assume. The writer of the pages was a woman who had come to Solomon's Cross and perhaps lived in this very house. She was from somewhere in Eastern Europe, and her family was trying to escape "the Enemy."

"Persecution or something," Jemma mused. She could not yet tell which part of Eastern Europe the woman had come from. The dates on the pages were blurred and faded with time, and she could make out a few of them.

November 1-, --51

De----er 25, 19-1

"November something, 1951?" she wondered. "And Christmas day, 1951 also?" Other days were even harder to read. Based on the context in the entries, this woman was writing about the aftermath of World War II. Jemma thought back to the board she had seen in Harv's Hamburgers and Hotcakes with the clippings and photographs from that war.

Her brows furrowed. What was this about? What did the journal entries have to do with the images in the photo album? Was the woman pictured there, this Eloise Brickell-wood, the one who had written these pages?

The difficulty of reading the script wasn't the only thing slowing down Jemma's progress. Either Tad had finished work much earlier than expected, or time had passed too quickly while Jemma was trying to transcribe. The front door creaked open, the hinges whining as Tad stepped in. His footsteps were heavy on the floorboards. Jemma jumped, but Tad didn't see her.

"Hey, Jem. You up there?"

Hurriedly, Jemma put the box of papers back into her closet. "Yes. I've just finished unpacking all my things." She didn't like lying to her father, but for some reason, she couldn't bring herself to share the stash of journal entries with anyone else yet, even with him. She poked her head over the edge of the loft and managed a greeting smile. "Are you home early?"

Tad's eyes twinkled. "Is that all right with you?" He waved a pamphlet. "I've got something to show you."

Jemma's heart sank. *Not the school talk again, please,* she thought, trying not to groan. She slid down the ladder and joined her father in the kitchen. He handed her the paper. Jemma's eyes widened. It was not about school, thank God.

The image on the front of the pamphlet showed a mountainside bed and breakfast called Gran's Rest. "They need someone to help with the grounds, Jem. This might not be your thing, but it might be worth investigating." He wiggled his eyebrows.

Jemma laughed and playfully slapped his arm with the paper. "Nancy Drew-style, eh? It's a job, not a case." She thought about the pile of Nancy Drew and Hardy Boys books in her loft. They were still in boxes. They had been a joy to read with her mother when she was younger, so she hadn't touched them in a few years.

Tad nudged her with his elbow. "Maybe you can find

out more about this town while you're working there. That's what I mean by investigating."

Jemma stilled. Her father had a point. "I'll call them and see about an interview."

Tad nodded and smiled. Jemma waited for him to bring up school, but he didn't, to her great relief. Instead, he turned slowly around in the kitchen, apparently searching for something. "What are you looking for?" she asked him.

Tad scratched the back of his head. "Oh…uh, it's nothing, Jem." He gave her a weak smile. "There's a whole hell of a lot to unpack, isn't there? I'm going to finish getting rid of all my boxes today."

He left the kitchen and went into his room. Jemma stayed behind, feeling strange. She wasn't the only one keeping secrets, it seemed. She was certain her father had been looking for the box full of memories from his marriage that was hidden in her closet. Jemma had seen him rifling through things in the garage a few days before. Even then, he hadn't told her what he was looking for. He wasn't giving up his search.

Jemma shook her head. "I wish he would," she whispered. "I wish we could forget all about her."

"Promise me you'll eat this," Jemma commanded as she set a sandwich on her father's desk. It was the Monday after she started transcribing the journals. She hadn't touched them since, and she was excited to get out of the house and go to Gran's Rest to see about the job. Calling had done nothing. The phone line seemed to be dead. Either that or the phone number listed on the pamphlet was no longer the correct one.

Jemma had finished school, eaten lunch, and made her father something to eat.

Tad looked up, grinning. "Promise me you didn't put mayo on it. Mayo is the devil's condiment."

Jemma rolled her eyes. "No mayo. Eat."

"Yes, ma'am."

She waved goodbye and headed out into the sun. The days were cooler now. The heat of summer had finally gone away. Cool mountain air whistled through the tall pines, rustling her auburn hair. Jemma had traded her sweatshirt for a denim jacket so she could be warm and comfortable but show a semblance of professionalism as well.

The walk took forty-five minutes, which she didn't mind. She hoped she would soon be able to get a bike and make the trip in less time. She appreciated the cool air when the walk became a continuous incline. The sun peeked through the clouds and beamed down on her. It didn't matter how cool it was because with the sun and the exertion, she arrived at the top of the hill flushed and sweating.

Jemma stopped short. What she faced wasn't quite a mountain but also not like the hikes she used to take in Indiana. Other mountains rose around her, so heavy with fog and mist that they were nearly obscured from view. "It's a wonder if anyone ever stays here," Jemma muttered as she scanned the area. The sign for Gran's Rest had almost been consumed by vines and weeds. The gravel walk was narrow and rutted. There seemed to be little space for parking, and the building, a large cabin-style structure, appeared desolate.

Aspects of it looked as ancient as the gnarled trees around it, but other parts were modern—the front door, the windows, and the porch swing. The roof appeared to have new shingles. Everything else, however, looked like it was centuries old. The walkway to the porch was so tangled with creepers and vines that it was treacherous.

"They sure as hell do need someone to take care of the grounds," Jemma grumbled. "Am I supposed to do all this shit?" She didn't know what taking care of the grounds even meant. Unsure about the whole situation, she considered turning back. "But do I want to trek back and tell Tad I didn't even bother to ask?" She shook her head and finished the walk to the porch.

When she put her foot on the sagging steps, she saw a movement from the corner of her eye. She turned and was startled. She cried out, and a hand flew to her mouth. The figure on the porch swing was bent and old and blended in with the exterior wall of the bed and breakfast so well that Jemma hadn't seen her. "I'm so sorry! I didn't see you there," she wheezed.

The crone, which was what she appeared to be, chuckled, then extended a thin, wrinkled hand and beckoned the newcomer forward. "Don't be sorry, dearie," she croaked. "It is I who should apologize. I saw you down by the sign and said not a word nor gave a single warning." She laughed as if the situation amused her very much.

Jemma did not share her amusement. "I'm looking for whoever is in charge of hiring around here. Would you know anything about—"

The old woman waved a hand to silence her. Jemma's mouth snapped shut, and irritation rose within her. The figure on the swing rose and wobbled over. When she stepped into the sunlight, she struck Jemma as being vaguely familiar. The woman's form was different, but her eyes had a wisdom and sternness she had seen before, though not in the person standing before her. These were the eyes that had stared at her from the pages of the photo album.

"You're Mrs. Eloise Brickellwood, aren't you?" Jemma asked, remembering what the town's people had said about the decrepit, seemingly immortal woman. She thought about her father. Had Tad known Mrs. Brickellwood was at Gran's Rest? Was that what he'd meant by "investigating?"

Mrs. Brickellwood's eyes twinkled, and she clucked while wagging a finger, "You've heard things, haven't you, dearie?" Tilting her head, she added, "I've never seen you before, have I?"

Jemma shrugged. "Not that I know of."

"Yet you seem familiar to me."

I could say the same thing, Jemma thought. She observed the old woman for a moment. Mrs. Eloise Brickellwood seemed far from the intimidating figure she was made out to be in the photos, but perhaps she had been younger and more full of life then. *The people at Harv's said she's been an old woman since many of them were children*, Jemma remembered. *It doesn't make any sense.*

Mrs. Brickellwood addressed her again in a gentle voice. "I need someone who can help me keep the place in order. Gardening and landscaping especially." She waved her hand at the grounds. Jemma had very little experience in gardening. This was not a job she was qualified to take.

"Look, Mrs. Brickellwood, I'm sorry, but I don't think I'm the one for this kind of job."

Another wave of the old woman's hand dismissed her refusal. "Call me Mama B, please, dearie. No problem about experience. I can teach you."

Jemma had her doubts. This old woman, who seemed like she could barely walk, was supposed to show her how to turn these weed-infested acres on the side of a mountain into respectable-looking grounds for a bed and breakfast? She wasn't able to keep her doubts from showing on her face. The old woman glanced at her and chuckled. She patted Jemma's hand before turning to the front door of the large cabin.

"Well, when do you want me to start?" Jemma asked.

The old woman opened the door and started to go inside. She seemed to have no intention of inviting Jemma to follow. "Tomorrow, dearie, and bring that old photo album you found. I've missed the thing more than I can say."

Jemma froze, shock keeping her rooted to her spot on the porch. How the hell had the old woman known she had it? Even if the photo album had pictures of Mrs. Brickellwood in it, how did she know Jemma had found it?

"How did you—" she started.

That waving hand of dismissal came again. "Oh, you know how people talk." The old woman turned so she could eye Jemma. "If you don't know, you will soon enough."

Had people from town come up here and told Mrs.

Brickellwood about the newcomers? Jemma doubted it. The people in Harv's diner had seemed afraid of the woman at Gran's Rest.

Further, Mrs. Brickellwood looked like she hadn't left her home in decades, and the grounds weren't very inviting. It was a wonder she had *any* visitors. For all Jemma knew, she was the first person to come here in a very long time.

I'm being silly and suspicious for no reason, Jemma told herself.

Without another word, Mrs. Eloise Brickellwood disappeared into the cabin, leaving Jemma alone on the porch. She turned as the reddening sun touched her flushed cheeks and ruffled her hair. She wasn't used to the sun setting early yet. Being in the mountains meant the sun disappeared faster since it slid behind the great rocks before it went behind the horizon.

Jemma took a deep breath. "Best I get back before it's dark," she muttered and set off down the hill, her mind swimming with questions and confusion.

CHAPTER FOUR

Jemma appreciated the downward slope as opposed to the steep incline she had defeated a couple of hours before. She was wary of the growing dusk, however.

"You're too old for childish fears of being out in the dark," she told herself. She was breathless as she made her way down the hill. The sun was sinking behind the mountains, tinting the edges of the great rocks red. The cool wind of night drifted in. She was no longer flushed and sweating as she made the trek.

She thought about the many things that came with the dark. She would have to be careful not to step on snakes. It wasn't the wildlife that made her shudder, though. The trees seemed to lean in as if they were closing over her. The rustling wind sounded like a soft, sighing breath. Neither helped matters.

As the reds turned to purples and the shadows lengthened and thickened, Jemma decided that seeing any vestige of civilization would do her good. The stretch of the rough road and leaning woods seemed to go on forever. Twigs snapped under her feet. Jemma stopped short. "Shit," she hissed. She had long since reached the bottom of the hill and had been walking straight for some time. She realized she didn't know where the hell she was. The woods and the road looked different now than they had during the day. She wasn't familiar enough with this area to know if she was going in the right direction.

She looked at the hill and the last of the sun leaking across the sky above it. "If I'm lost, I'm going to lose my fucking mind." She pulled in a deep breath of cool air and continued walking. Going straight down the road seemed to be the only possibility.

Without warning, the muddy, rutted road turned into pavement, and pools of light from streetlights shone on the cement ahead. She heard noises up ahead as well—low voices and the steady rumble of a car that turned off a second later. Jemma Nox was no longer alone in the twilight.

Huddled close to the road in front of a long-abandoned fishing and tackle shop were two vehicles, and they couldn't have been more different from one another. One was an old beater truck that was just a hunk of rust with a motor, and the other was a slick, shining sports car. Their headlights were on and cast even more light on the road. The forest behind the fishing and tackle shack loomed large and dark. Jemma was thankful to be out of it but not sure how she felt about her new surroundings.

The top of the sports car was down, revealing the faces of two youths about Jemma's age. The bed of the truck also held three or four people; she couldn't quite tell in the shadows. They appeared to be drinking and smoking, but their commotion was contained. It didn't seem to matter how loud they were being, though. This place was far from anyone's house. They wouldn't disturb anyone with their noise here.

So, I've stumbled upon one of the local hangouts, Jemma mused to herself. *Are they having a party? Weird for a Monday night.*

She stepped closer but stayed in the shadows. She didn't want to be seen. The hangout looked boring even for Solomon's Cross, but she soon realized that if this was a party, she was it. Jemma had stepped into the light without realizing it, and as her feet crunched on gravel and twigs, eyes slid in her direction.

"Who is that?" one of the girls in the back of the truck asked.

"Don't know," someone else answered. "Never seen her before. She new 'round here, ya think?"

"You seen her at school?" a young man asked his friend. The answer was "no," but Jemma didn't hear if that was the response or not.

There were more low murmurs. Jemma stood stock-still, unsure of what to do. She couldn't just disappear back into the forest. She'd have to pass them and hope they didn't stop her. Her dread grew, and she set off down the road without casting another glance at the kids as quickly as she could without running. As she passed the group, however, she realized they didn't intend to let her go quietly.

"Hey, you!" one of them shouted.

Shit! Jemma thought. She halted and slowly turned to face them.

The group, which was comprised of seven or eight individuals, got out of the truck and the car and approached her. Jemma wouldn't be able to avoid them without making it obvious that was what she was doing. Run and embarrass herself or stick around and trudge through tortuous small talk? She weighed her options silently.

The choice was made for her. The youths formed a semi-circle around her, trapping her between them and the part of the road that dropped into a small gorge. Deep within her, Jemma had the irrational yet sincere fear that what was happening here was like what a witch would experience before villagers seized her and dragged her off to the stake.

The teens of Solomon Cross observed her with narrowed eyes and expressions of interest. Although a couple of them sized her up like prey, most looked curious. Her previous fears about being dragged off faded when they finally addressed her and she learned their intentions were quite the opposite of her earlier assumption.

"You just come all the way from Gran's Rest?" a boy with red hair and freckles asked. He looked no older than Jemma. "On foot?" His eyes were wide with awe. The others stirred, casting curious glances at her as if they too were amazed by her achievement.

"Well," Jemma started, finding it difficult to speak, "yes."

The teens gave one another knowing glances. Low murmurs and shrugs followed.

"Huh," one of the girls, who had a purple streak in her dark hair, muttered. "Impressive."

Jemma's brows furrowed. She didn't see why it was, but the consensus agreed with the speaker's sentiment.

"We saw you goin' up the road and waited to see if you'd come back," the ginger told her. "We didn't think you would." He shifted uncomfortably. "Can't say any of us would have followed you, either." He chuckled.

Nice, Jemma thought. Good to know everyone here is willing to help someone they think is in danger. Her doubt showed on her face.

Her peers pressed forward, seemingly unaware that they were closing in around her. Their questions clamored over one another. "How did you do it? How did you escape?"

"Did she cast a spell on you or some shit?"

"How far did the damn witch chase you before you got away?"

Witch? She's not a witch! was all Jemma could think. The questions overwhelmed her before she could form an answer.

"It's not every day someone escapes the clutches of a full-blown, child-eating, hex-hurling monstrous hag, ya know?" the girl with the purple streak remarked.

What the fuck? Compared to the Mama B she had met, the description was as hilariously fanciful as it was woefully inaccurate. Mrs. Brickellwood was right; people did talk. Jemma was finding that out quickly, as the old woman had promised.

Instinctually, she stumbled back to get away from them. Her peers stopped short. "Give her some space," the ginger told his friends. They stepped back, much to Jemma's relief. They weren't trying to scare her. They were just eager for answers. She was eager for answers, too.

None of the kids looked younger than sixteen. Some looked like they were not teenagers but in their early twenties.

For an instant, Jemma considered playing to their dramatic story. She could hold their attention by making up a good story for them. Then who would they talk about, the new girl in town who made it out of a witch's clutches? Jemma shook her thoughts away. It wasn't who she was.

Back in Hendricks, Indiana, she had been the subject of much attention after her mother left. She was called a "poor dear" and lectured for choosing her "broke father over a mother as nice as Delilah." The feelings Jemma had experienced then came rushing back as she faced the youths in her new town.

Jemma forced these thoughts away and laughed. "She's not like that." She shrugged. "Just a sweet old lady." She hesitated, then added, "She's giving me a job. Been hard to find one around here."

Their disappointment was palpable. Jemma could sense it curdling into hostility toward her. Someone at the back of the group muttered, "My momma says she seen the witch runnin' through the woods. You callin' my momma a liar?"

"Yeah, I've seen some shit too," the ginger at the front remarked, his expression turning hard.

Jemma stumbled back, hands forward in defense. "Look, I don't know. I just…" Her words trailed off. A lump formed in her throat. Her heart had been pounding a little harder since leaving Gran's Rest, but now it hammered in her chest.

Before things could go too far, a soft but firm voice spoke up from the middle of the group. A figure with thin dark hair stepped forward. The others parted around the girl. Jemma looked at her with wide eyes. "Unless any of y'all are goin' back up the hill to Gran's Rest to look for yourself, you have no right to call this girl a liar." She cast sharp glances at her companions.

Jemma felt a combination of relief and confusion. The girl standing before her appeared sickly. Her hair looked like it was falling out. Though she was a little older than Jemma, her shrunken frame and bowed posture made her look small and, therefore, much younger. Her frail body didn't seem capable of speaking with such force, but her voice had steel in it. Everyone shifted and shared looks. Whoever this girl was, the others listened to her. She commanded attention and respect just by standing among them.

The girl's eyes, dark and restless, met Jemma's. Her thin, pale lips parted to say something. Perhaps she was going to introduce herself, but she was interrupted. A deep, drawling voice filled the space, wrenching everyone's attention, especially Jemma's, to the person it came from. "Hey now, Easter. Let's not get ahead of ourselves."

Easter must have been the name of the girl who had spoken.

The deep, raspy voice belonged to a tall, lean youth dressed in oil-stained jeans and a white tank top. He moved with strength and litheness, sinew and hunger in one sleek package.

Jemma couldn't take her eyes off him. She could only drink in his every feature in riveted silence. He had dark hair, ice-blue eyes, and a sly smirk parting his lips. Between his teeth was a cigarette, which he removed with two fingers. He blew the blue-gray vapor in the direction of the sickly-looking girl, who covered her nose with a handkerchief and coughed.

The young man's eyes slid from the girl he had addressed as Easter to Jemma. "We weren't at the top of that God-forsaken hill, you're right, but I find it funny that you came back with nothing but some mud on your boots." His eyes traveled down her body. Jemma stiffened. She hated this guy already. She hated how he looked. She hated his voice and his smirk and his cigarette and how he had blown smoke into the other girl's face.

He cocked his head, the sly grin on his lips growing wider. "Maybe New Girl here made a deal with the witch. Maybe the old crone let her come back to spread the word that it's safe up there. Hell, for all we know, she could be in cahoots with the old woman. Weren't you the one who came into Harv's with some pictures, wonderin' about the old hag? What if you were tryin' to get us all to talk?" He gestured at his companions. The previously curious and open expressions had turned suspicious. Wary glances passed over Jemma. Eyes narrowed. Shoulders stiffened.

The young man chuckled darkly and puffed his cigarette, this time blowing the smoke at Jemma. She wanted to punch the guy in the nose, but she already looked guilty. Punching someone twice her size was a very bad idea.

"You're just being fucking stupid, AJ," Easter retorted. "Pick on someone your own size, why don't you?"

AJ turned on the girl. "Oh, someone like you?" He poked her shoulder and loomed over the girl like a bending tree. Indignation swelled within Jemma. She saw the same feeling written all over Easter's face. The indignation turned to flickering hurt when AJ next spoke. "Just because you're dying doesn't mean the rest of us don't have something to live for. We have a future and need to watch for danger." He whirled on Jemma. "Like some city girl teaming up with a witch."

"The whole thing is fucking ridiculous," Jemma snapped before she thought to rein in her words. She immediately regretted them despite how true they were. Why was a city girl being in cahoots with a witch in a no-name mountain town a thing? Were these kids so bored that making up stories about strangers was a pastime?

AJ's lips curled back from his teeth. He snarled but didn't say a word.

The others around him had a similar reaction as her. "Come on now, AJ, don't talk to Easter like that. That's beneath even you," the girl with the purple streak in her hair drawled. Other voices chimed in, trying to calm the tall young man down.

Jemma's hands clenched into fists at her side. Easter's dark, serious eyes remained on her adversary. She had a feeling this wasn't the first time these two had locked horns. The tension was thick but didn't feel unfamiliar. Those standing around AJ and Easter didn't seem to be taking the situation seriously, but there was one who didn't act so nonchalantly. Another young man, the smallest of them, stepped forward.

Jemma was struck by the similarity between him and Easter. Her brother, maybe? He had the same dark features and serious eyes. Although he didn't look ill like she did, he was smaller and thinner than the other boys.

"Shut the fuck up, AJ," he demanded in his cracking teenage voice. "I won't stand for that kind of talk about my damn sister." Jemma was surprised by the ferocity in his tone, not because of the sense behind his words, but because AJ was much larger than he was.

"Aw, fuck off, Val. Pick a fight that isn't about your sister for once, why don't you?" AJ taunted as he flung a much longer arm forward and shoved Easter's brother away.

"Val, no!" Easter cried as her brother bared his teeth and rushed the larger man. She couldn't manage more than a small cry with her weakened voice. She tried to grab his arm, but it was too late. He and AJ collided with Easter between them, and all three went down. Because of his longer limbs, AJ was able to get to his feet faster, leaving the two siblings tangled on the ground, wincing in pain.

Without thinking, eyes blazing and heart hammering, Jemma rushed toward AJ. She knew it wouldn't be a fair fight. He had every advantage over her: strength, reach, and weight. Plus, she had never been in a fight. This wasn't like her. What the hell was she doing? she wondered. She was too angry to stop her actions.

AJ didn't see her coming. He was too busy snarling at the fallen boy he had called Val. Jemma was there the next instant with a cut kick that slammed her shin into the young man's knee like a baseball bat. He was knocked off balance enough so that his head bowed forward, which gave her enough space to pivot her body and catch him across the jaw with her elbow.

She had never done this to anyone but her father before, and with him, it had been during martial arts lessons they had taken together. She never expected to use it on a guy like this on a road bordering the woods at night. If only Tad could see what a great job she was doing now at making friends! The whole ordeal was amusing since the guy she had hit was a total jackass.

Stunned, AJ reeled back and went down like a sack on the road. He clutched at his bleeding lip, and his hat popped off as his head rebounded off the pavement.

"Leave them alone!" Jemma shouted, fists clenched at her sides. She stood, panting and still hot with anger despite her surprise at her actions. She hoped to God AJ wouldn't get up and look for a further fight. The young man's clear advantages and scarred knuckles told her any further altercation was unlikely to turn out in her favor.

He climbed to his feet, cursing and looking around for his hat. He cast Jemma a venomous glare, more poisonous than any snake she'd encountered on the walk here. He didn't come toward her, though, since everyone else in the group leveled stony expressions at him. No one was happy about what he had said to Easter and Val.

The youth of Solomon's Cross had seemingly become used to AJ sneering at Easter's illness, whatever it was, but physical violence toward her and her brother was taking things too far.

The ginger patted AJ on the back. "Drunk too much tonight, I think, AJ. Let's go."

AJ's angry blue eyes didn't leave Jemma. *He's wondering what sort of damage his reputation will suffer for being beaten up by the new girl*, Jemma thought.

"I haven't drunk *enough*," AJ snarled at his friend as he snatched a can of beer from the other boy's hand and finished it off. "She's working with the witch to pick off the sick and weak ones, I'll bet," he muttered as he staggered toward his sports car. He hopped in and squealed away. The relief in the air after he was gone was palpable. Shoulders relaxed. Expressions softened. Easter and Val were helped up from the ground.

"Show's over, everyone," Purple Streak Girl announced. The rest disbanded in small groups and trudged down the road. Some of them had bikes and wheeled off.

Easter and Val hung behind.

Jemma stood before them, still panting. "Are you two all right?"

They nodded. "Thank you," Easter croaked. "You didn't need to do that."

Val rubbed his right arm. "Yes, thank you."

Jemma laughed nervously. "I should be thanking *you*." She extended a hand awkwardly. "My name is Jemma Nox."

A small smile appeared on the girl's lips. "Nice to meet you, Jemma. I'm Easter McCarthy. This is my brother Valentine."

"Call me Val," her brother offered with a little wave. "That motherfucker you met is Anthony Jean Kilmer. You'll hear his family's name around town. Best to stay away from the whole lot of them." For someone so small, Valentine McCarthy had bite and sting in his words.

"Let us take you home, please?" Easter asked Jemma. "As a thank you for doing that." She chuckled. "I've never seen AJ thrown down like that before."

Jemma's reputation, it seemed, was growing. She wasn't sure she liked that. No, she knew she didn't. She was unsettled, but part of her felt satisfied for dealing with the bully, too.

Easter nodded at the beater truck. "That's our ride. Val will drive."

Jemma gave the vehicle and then Val a wary look, not hiding her misgivings. Val looked closer to shoe-tying than license-having. There did not, however, seem to be a better option. Jemma didn't want to walk the rest of the way home in the dark, especially since she didn't know where the hell she was.

Seeing the look on Jemma's face, Easter laughed. "I promise the truck isn't any more dangerous than going up to Gran's Rest." She put enough spooky inflection into her voice to tell Jemma she was joking.

Jemma found, to her relief, that she liked Easter McCarthy and had some pity in her for Val. "Thanks. A ride home would be great."

CHAPTER FIVE

Jemma soon discovered that Easter couldn't drive because her medication, whatever it was, made her unsteady sometimes. "Might faint," she explained with a light laugh.

Jemma didn't know how to reply so she just offered a tight-lipped smile.

Val drove them down the twisting mountain road as if he had been doing it since he was born. Jemma found she had misjudged his driving abilities. Because he had grown up in this part of Tennessee, he was quite used to the mountain roads with all the twists and turns and close edges dropping off into gorges. Jemma's heart lurched into her throat as he took a particularly sharp turn at a much faster rate than she would have and in the dark, no less. Speeding on mountain roads, it seemed, was the norm around here. The signs warning of sharp bends were usually ignored.

Jemma clenched the armrest on the door. Easter noticed and chuckled. "Don't worry. Val is one of the safest drivers around here. AJ would have taken that turn at seventy." She laughed again. Jemma didn't find it amusing. She had barely been behind the wheel. She had started learning how to drive shortly after her mother left them, but with her father's depression that followed, she had put his needs before her own. She wasn't that disappointed. She wasn't very keen on driving through the mountains when she was used to the flatness of northern Indiana, comprised of interstate, suburbs, and corn fields.

Jemma watched the two siblings as they spoke in low voices to one another. She sat in the backseat. Easter said something that made Val laugh. The tension in his shoulders went away. The anger he had felt toward AJ seemed to slide off and be gone. Jemma felt a light mood enter the truck. At one point, Easter flipped on the radio. At this spot in the mountains, it was mostly static, but she could hear the distant voice of some country singer. Val sang along in a low voice while his sister hummed.

Her phone rang, startling her. *Geez,* she thought, *jumpy much?* It made sense after what she had been through. Aloud, she said into the phone, "Hey, Dad."

"Jem, where are you?" He sounded worried. "Are you okay? I didn't expect you to be gone so long."

"I'll be there in a few minutes, and yes, I'm all right." She took a deep breath and wondered if she was really all right. She was glad to have a ride and was physically in good condition, but the fight with AJ hadn't been processed yet.

"Okay, that's good, Jem. You should have called me and had me come pick you up," Tad replied.

"I got a ride, Dad. We'll be there soon."

"Who—" he started, but Jemma cut him off in the most cheerful-sounding voice she could manage.

"A couple of kids I met. Hey, Tad?"

"Yeah, Jem?"

"Promise me you won't start cooking when we get there?" Easter glanced back, confused but smiling.

Tad laughed. "Our fridge is empty. Otherwise, I would."

Jemma hung up, grinning at the memory of all the times she had come back from school with a friend to find her father trying to cook an extravagant dinner for them. She admired him for his hospitality, but the last thing she wanted after a long day was dinner with two people she had just met.

"You call your dad by his first name?" Easter asked, still looking into the backseat at Jemma.

Jemma nodded, still smiling. "Everyone calls him Tad. 'Mr. Nox' sounds weird, so don't feel like you have to call him that."

Easter's dark eyes gleamed. "Well, he'll fit in here just fine, then."

A hundred questions filled Jemma's mind. She wanted to know more about the McCarthy siblings. She wanted to know about their parents, and if they liked the school they went to. Did they have jobs? She settled for asking, "So, how long have you two lived in Solomon's Cross?"

"Since the womb," Val announced. "Never left." His hands clenched the steering wheel. "Though I wouldn't be mad if we did." His hardened tone returned. He spoke as if he couldn't leave even if he wanted to.

Easter laid a comforting hand on his arm. "Gets a little smaller the longer you're here, ya know?" She looked at Jemma. "You'll feel it eventually."

What Jemma didn't say was that she felt it already. The

mountains, as large as they were, seemed to close the whole town in, trapping her there with dingy diners, tall pine trees, and stories about a witch who was just a sweet old woman.

She looked at Val. "Where would you go if you left?"

Val shared a glance with his sister. Some silent interchange took place that Jemma wasn't a part of. Then he shrugged. "Don't know. Anywhere, I think. Anywhere that isn't here."

Jemma sighed. "That's exactly how I felt when I left Indiana. I wanted to go any place where I wouldn't run into my mother." She hadn't planned on saying so much out loud. It kind of came out. Perhaps these two new acquaintances made it easy for her to share things about herself.

Easter gave her a sincere look. "Sounds like a shitty time."

Jemma nodded. "Yeah, pretty shitty." She shifted, looking out the window. "We're here." Through the pine trees appeared a gravel drive, then Jemma and Tad Nox's newly acquired home. The door opened and light flooded onto the porch. Val pulled the truck to a stop but kept it running. Jemma hopped from the back.

Tad came out the front door, wearing a broad smile as his eyes alighted on the two people sitting in the front of the truck. "Thanks for the ride. I appreciate it," Jemma told Val and Easter.

"No problem," Easter responded, smiling. It was as if getting to know Jemma had allowed her to forget the nastiness of the encounter with AJ Kilmer.

"Any time," Val added. "You don't wanna walk in the woods by yourself. Not at night, anyway."

Tad approached them. "Hey there. Thanks for giving Jem a ride home." He had no idea what had happened, but that didn't stop him from being friendly from the start. "I'm Tad. Nice to meet you both."

Easter and Val responded warmly. Easter introduced herself and then her younger brother. She winked at Tad. "It wouldn't be a good idea to have Jemma walk home from work every day if she ends up working at Gran's Rest."

During the drive, Jemma had been so preoccupied with getting to know the McCarthys that she had almost forgotten the events preceding their meeting. "We'll be going now," Easter added. "Hope we'll see you around, Jemma."

Jemma gave a genuine smile. As the siblings drove off, she had the feeling that she had met her first friends in Solomon's Cross. She turned to find her father beaming with pride. "I knew you could do it, Jem! Do they work at Gran's Rest too?"

Jemma sighed. "Quite the opposite. It seems like everyone is afraid of the old lady who lives up there."

Tad put his arm around his daughter. "You can tell me all about it while we eat dinner. I ordered pizza. I hope that's okay."

They walked into the house, and as soon as Tad closed the door, he said, "I was worried when you pulled up in a truck with people I didn't recognize, but once I saw them, that went away." He chuckled. "The girl looks like she could barely keep her head up, poor thing, and her brother could drown in a short glass of water."

Knowing he meant well, Jemma grinned.

Tad grinned back, poking his daughter in the shoulder. "Knowing as I do about your impressive martial arts abilities, I'm not too worried. They seem like nice people."

Jemma's grin faded as she recalled the altercation with AJ Kilmer. She was on the edge of a slippery slope, the one where she would hide another thing from her father. Jemma shook her head. She didn't want the lies to pile up.

Tad handed her a plate with two slices of pepperoni pizza on it, and Jemma began to explain all that had happened, starting with her trek up the mountain to Gran's Rest. His brows furrowed at the mention of the photo album. "I swear I didn't mention it. She just *knew* somehow," Jemma insisted.

Tad sat down. "She's Mrs. Eloise Brickellwood, right?"

Jemma nodded. "The very one in the photo album. Much older, like everyone at Harv's said she was. She knows where we live." She shook her head. "I don't understand it."

Tad began to eat. "What happened next?"

"Well, she told me to come back tomorrow to start work. I don't get it. I don't know what we're going to be doing, but I'm going anyway."

"So, you left after that?"

Jemma nodded. "The sun was going down." She described her run-in with the teens of Solomon Cross. Tad was amused at the kids' spouting of urban legends regarding Mrs. Eloise Brickellwood. His amusement faded, however, when Jemma explained the part involving AJ Kilmer. She hesitated when she talked about throwing her elbow into the guy's jaw. Sure, her father had taught her how to defend herself, but that had never involved her starting a fight. It wasn't like her.

Tad's eyes held conflicting emotions, surprise at his daughter for punching a guy much bigger than her and anger at the guy for needing to be punched. If Jemma Nox, his only daughter, thought the young man needed to bleed a little and did it herself, it was a big deal. Jemma didn't like approaching people for conversation, much less a fight.

Tad's eyes raked over her, looking for signs of retaliation. "I'm fine, Tad. He didn't do anything to me."

Her dad's fists clenched. "I don't care. I'll hang him by his scrotum from the nearest tree."

Jemma sighed. She'd guessed this would be his reaction. "It's over, Tad. It happened quickly, and he didn't even threaten me before he left. I doubt we'll have a run-in like this again." She said it but was far from convinced it was true. She lived in a small town and planned on seeing Easter and Val again. AJ might have even been one of the guys smoking on the side of the street that first night they'd gone to Harv's diner.

Jemma squeezed her father's arm. "I don't want my Poppa Bear to go around mauling teenagers I've already beaten up." She laughed at her own words. Tad frowned for a second but then broke into a grin as well.

He patted Jemma's hand. "I knew I taught you martial arts for a reason." His features softened. "Congratulations on getting a job, by the way. I know finding one has been hard." He smiled. "If you want, I'd be more than happy to drive you there in the morning."

Jemma nodded. "I'd like that." Her mind was stuck on his "I know finding a job has been hard" statement. She hadn't shared that with him, but somehow, Tad had been able to tell. That was how their relationship worked; they knew what was wrong even when the other didn't want to say anything.

"We'll be starting new routines now that we're here," Tad remarked as he finished his first slice of pizza and took a drink. "But that doesn't mean we have to give up all our old ones."

Jemma grinned. "I don't think there are any options for martial arts classes around here."

Tad shrugged, and his eyes glittered. "Maybe I can teach one of my own."

Jemma doubted that, and it showed on her face. She took her dishes to the sink and began to wash them. "We had fun in Mr. Wu's class, Tad, but I don't think you can remake that experience."

Tad turned solemn. "I think you're right. We can't remake it. We always had classes after you were done with school and then went home, where your mother had dinner made, and…" His words trailed off. Jemma turned to see his face engulfed with memories.

She set the soapy dish down and wiped her hands. She was caught off-guard by how quickly her father sank back into his depression. Helplessness flooded through her. She didn't have a damn clue what to do about it. Jemma Nox was tired of battling the darkness that enfolded the two of them at any mention or memory of Delilah. *Damn you, Delilah,* she wanted to hiss, but saying her mother's name would bring pain to her father.

"We lead a not-so-normal life, don't we?" Before she could answer, Tad leaned forward, the lines of his face deepened by the creeping depression. "Hey, Jem, any chance you've seen that box with all the letters and pictures?" He asked the question hesitantly.

Jemma felt a flash of anger. Her expression hardened. The last thing she needed was for her father to regress. "No, I haven't seen it," she answered tightly, "and if I had, I would have burned it." Tad looked up at her, brows knitting together. She forged on. "We promised to be done with all that. That's why we came here."

Tad nodded. "I know. You're right."

Jemma found she had been clenching the dishtowel as she spoke. She softened her hold and tried to relax. She realized the ferocity of her voice had hurt him. He wouldn't look at her. *Shit*, she thought, trying to find a way to repair things. Delilah had done enough damage. She didn't need to come between father and daughter now that they were away from her.

Tad didn't give his daughter a chance for repairs. He rose from the table. "I'm feeling awful tired, Jem. I'll see you tomorrow when I take you to work."

Jemma watched her father trudge out of the kitchen. She felt sick to her stomach. The sharp sniffs coming from her father as he went into his room told her he was trying not to cry. It was almost enough to send her rushing to her closet to get the offending box and come clean. She shook her head and turned back to the dishes. She feared the consequences of the lie, though.

But it'll poison him too. He can't know, she determined. Jemma finished the dishes and headed to the loft, head throbbing from the emotional ups and downs of the day.

She climbed into bed, hoping tomorrow would be less exciting.

She wanted to live a normal life in Solomon's Cross, Tennessee. She tried to ignore the feeling in the back of her mind that told her such a thing wouldn't be possible.

CHAPTER SIX

Jemma awoke to the pale light of morning filtering through the curtainless windows. The house was in desperate need of some sprucing up and decorating. First, though, she had to start her new job. Once dressed and down the ladder, she found her father in the kitchen.

Tad was more soft-spoken than usual that morning. Jemma took it as a sign that he was still embarrassed about his behavior from the night before. It didn't make Jemma feel better, but she didn't know how to handle the situation. "Might rain today," she remarked over breakfast.

Tad nodded.

Fuck this, she thought. *I don't want to resort to talking about the weather with my father.* She glanced through one of the front windows. It was overcast, but as they finished eating the eggs Tad had prepared, the sun peeked from behind the clouds. Jemma hoped it wouldn't be a hot day since she expected to be outside for the majority of her time at Gran's Rest.

Tad seemed to be in a better mood by the time they

hopped into the truck and rode up the mountain to the secluded bed and breakfast. All of Jemma's questions from the day before came flooding back. She carried the photo album in her backpack.

Tad frowned as he drove up the incline. "A bit overgrown, isn't it?" He raised his brows and eyed Jemma. He didn't voice his concerns about the job, but Jemma shared them. She had never taken care of land before, much less a whole property that was supposed to welcome overnight guests. "I wonder when the last time someone other than the owner stayed here was?" Tad added.

Jemma had wondered the same thing. Her father pulled to a stop, and both of them got out. Like the day before, Mrs. Brickellwood sat on the porch. Like Jemma when she first met the old woman, Tad didn't see her at first. When they came closer, he started. "Sorry, ma'am. Didn't see you there." He stepped forward as she rose and extended a hand. She shook it, chuckling as she looked him over.

"This is my dad, Tad Nox," Jemma introduced him.

"Ah, I know that, dearie." The old woman clucked. "Come to drop ye off on yer first day." She turned to Tad. "Call me Mama B, if you would. No ma'ams or Mrs. needed around here, sir."

"Then call me Tad," Jemma's dad replied, rocking back on his heels and smiling broadly. "No sirs necessary. Everyone calls me Tad, even my daughter." He ruffled Jemma's hair with one hand. She didn't like it since it made her feel like a little kid, but she made no verbal objection. Tad saw the look on her face and put both hands in his pockets.

He turned to his daughter. "Well, I'll be off now. Pick you up at, err, what time?"

"I'll call you," Jemma replied, giving him a reassuring smile.

Tad moved off, and a moment later, he was backing down the hill.

Jemma watched him go with a strange feeling in her chest. He had forced out his friendly nature in the encounter with Mama B, but Jemma knew their conversation from the previous night still weighed on him. She turned to the old woman, who was peering at the road where Tad's truck had just been. "How long has he been down like that?" she asked.

Jemma struggled to answer. She wasn't sure how the old woman could have known that since she had just met the man. "He's having a bad morning. Happens to all of us, doesn't it?" she replied in as cheerful a voice as she could muster. "Can we talk about what days you'll need me here? I'm doing school at home, so I'm pretty flexible, but if you could tell me—"

Being interrupted by Mama B's waving hand seemed like it would be a regular occurrence. "Don't you worry about that, child. We'll start now and figure it out as we go."

Jemma wasn't a fan of uncertainty, but she followed the old woman without another question. Mama B shuffled off the porch and around the large house to the back, where the yard extended for several acres before it dropped off down another incline. The mountains rose in the distance, heavy fog lying over them. The sun was beginning to fill the land with golden light. The fog made the sunlight hazy. Jemma soaked in the view, breathless and awed.

Mama B gestured at the land around them. "Look at all this, child. Look at this and tell me what it tells you."

Jemma's brows furrowed. What the hell did this old woman mean? "I don't know," she replied.

Mama B was patient. She laid a warm hand on Jemma's arm. "All this means we have to trust one another. We're helping each other, girl, and that means we have to trust each other."

Confusion flickered across Jemma's face. It wasn't that she disagreed with the sentiment. She didn't understand its purpose. The old woman shuffled through the overgrown weeds to a stone bench. In front of the bench was a fountain. The base was cracked but still together. A figure of an angel was at the top. Water trickled into little pools in its base.

Mama B sat on the bench and patted the spot next to her for Jemma to take a seat as well. "Tell me all about yourself."

Jemma hesitated, wondering how much of her history the old woman already knew since she seemed to have some knowledge about the photo album and could see her father's true emotions even when he attempted to mask them. *Just tell her. Be open and honest like she asked,* Jemma told herself.

"My father Tad and I moved here a few weeks ago from Hendricks, Indiana. We moved because...well, the short version is, my mother left us but didn't leave the area we all lived in. It became too much, seeing her everywhere. Too much for both of us." Mama B listened without judgment and nodded, not making any comments.

The dam burst. Jemma started spilling details about her childhood to this point that she hadn't thought about in years. It all just came out. Something about the old woman's presence made it easy. She told Mama B about the friends she had had in elementary school who became more like strangers by the time her mother left when Jemma was in high school. She told her about the places in Hendricks she missed but never wanted to go back to despite that.

Why am I telling her all this? Jemma wondered. She stopped talking, realizing she had gone on for far longer than she'd intended. It wasn't that she wanted to keep secrets, but she'd never shared this much with anyone before.

Mama B patted her hand. "Very good. Now, we better get to work." She heaved herself to her feet.

That's it? Jemma thought. Nothing from her? She reached for her backpack. "Wait. I have something to ask you about the photo album. I brought it like you asked."

Mama B shot her a sidelong glance. Slowly, Jemma drew the object of interest from her bag. The old woman eyed it before waving her hand. "Another time, maybe." She moved away from the bench.

Jemma sat with her mouth hanging open. She had just spilled her whole life's story to this woman, only to receive very little response. Now she didn't even want to talk about the photo album? She was perplexed. It looked like Mama B was bound and determined to get to work. She got up and followed her.

Jemma spent the first half of the day learning how to differentiate between the various plants on the property. "I'm not sure why I have to learn what is what since I'm going to be getting rid of them eventually," she muttered as she trailed several paces behind the old woman, hoping she wouldn't hear her.

Jemma soon discovered she didn't know a damn thing about botany. The task before her wasn't going to involve only landscaping; this was about herbal remedies as well. Except for the weeds, vines, and moss sprouting everywhere, almost every small plant was procured and saved by the old woman for its "medicinal benefits."

Some of them sounded reasonable, but others, Jemma had her doubts about. At one point, Mama B bent down at the edge of a stone path and pointed out different plants to her young apprentice. One was a cluster of drooping purple flowers. "Comfrey," Mama B told her. "Used to mend broken bones."

Jemma's brows rose. She didn't know it was possible to do that with plants.

"It looks much like foxglove, but they are not the same. Foxglove is poison if ingested." The old woman pointed at a clump of red clover, a plant Jemma recognized. "Good for purifying the blood, especially in women." She grasped the roots firmly and pulled them up before putting the plant in Jemma's hand. "Take some home." She spoke as if the whole thing was the most delightful event ever to happen to her. Jemma's heart expanded. Perhaps this old woman had been alone for a very long time. Maybe she didn't care so much about the grounds. Maybe she just wanted company.

Other explanations sounded less reasonable to Jemma and more along the lines of esoteric or magical. *It's a down-home flourish,* Jemma thought. *It sounds better to explain it like that.*

Mama B shuffled on down the path but stopped short before it went over the slope. She bent down, beckoning Jemma to look closely with her. "See this? Mugwort."

The plant she pointed at looked like thin, sprawling weeds, no different than what shot up at the front of the house. Jemma nodded even though she was unable to see the difference.

"Combine this with rue to keep the haints away." Mama B chuckled.

Jemma frowned, unsure of her meaning.

"The boo hags get sick at the scent of dill." The old woman continued to mutter incoherently, chuckling to herself now and then. Jemma had no damn clue what "haints" and "boo hags" were, but she was determined to believe Mama B's explanations were not instructions for magical workings.

They couldn't be. She was being too matter-of-fact about all of it.

At long last, they began the kind of work Jemma had been expecting: clearing the excess and undesired plants. It was the second half of the day when they began this work. The fog lifted, and the sun emerged in her full glory.

True to her word, Mama B was by Jemma's side through the whole process, providing helpful hints that made the job a little easier along the way. Sometimes it was showing Jemma how to best pull the roots of some stubborn weed from the ground. Other times it was a suggestion on how to bundle and tie the leavings of their labors to get them put away.

When their work ended for the day, Jemma was surprised by how much they had gotten done. Even though it had wearied her, it had been easier than she had anticipated. "Perhaps I have a bright and shining future in grounds work."

She laughed to herself as she stood, hands braced on her hips, and surveyed their work. She and Mama B stood in the front yard of the property. The weeds, which had grown over the path, had been cleared, leaving an easy route to the porch and the front door. Tomorrow, she was told, they would clear all the weeds that had grown up around the porch.

Jemma stood still for a moment and caught her breath. She found to both her surprise and her relief that she was looking forward to it. A long day of work in the sun did one good sometimes. She glanced at the old woman and realized something peculiar: Mama B had kept up with her the entire time. Not once had she shown signs of fatigue or asked to take a break. Her breathing had come easily, and her hands were steady and sure. The old woman was not as feeble as she appeared.

"Go get your things, dearie," Mama B instructed the young girl. Covered in dirt and sweat but not caring, Jemma went to the back of the house to get her backpack. Mama B followed. They stood for a moment, looking over the back portion of the property. There was a good deal to do in the garden, but Jemma was no longer daunted by the prospect.

The old woman gestured at the slope at the rear of the

house. "I used to have evening dinners for guests here. This will require a lot of attention if we're to get it back to the way it was." She chuckled. "We wouldn't want the guests to have to eat among the weeds, now would we?"

Jemma's eyes widened. Did Mrs. Brickellwood intend to open this place back up? She wondered how long it has been in this state of disarray. She tried to picture a time when this place was populated and picturesque. She imagined strings of lights hanging from the boughs of the great trees and flowers growing on either side of the stone path. She imagined the sound of the fountain bubbling and guests chattering with clinking glasses. It was difficult to believe this place had ever been like that.

What had happened?

Her thoughts faded as the sound of truck tires on the gravel drive reached her ears. *Tad's here.* She picked up her backpack and followed the old woman around to the front of the house. The sun had nearly vanished over the side of the mountain, leaving the sky stained with an array of dark colors: wine red, purple like bruises, and a faded blush pink.

Tad hopped out of the driver's seat after pulling the truck to a stop. He looked much calmer than he had this morning. He placed his hands on his hips and surveyed the front yard. "It looks like you two made quite a lot of progress!" He sounded happy about it. He surveyed his daughter as she approached him. "And you look like you need a bath." He chuckled and ruffled her hair as if she were much younger than sixteen.

"A well-deserved one, Tad," Jemma answered. "It was a good day of work."

"I can see that." His eyes glittered. Jemma felt warm inside. Perhaps their conversation from the night before could be forgotten.

Mama B hobbled over. "Your daughter is doing quite well. As a reward for her first day of work, I'll give you both something sweet. I noticed the supply of sweets you keep in your bag there." She pointed at Jemma's backpack. When Jemma had pulled out the photo album, perhaps the old woman had seen the many candy wrappers inside.

Mama B winked and shuffled into the house. She was gone for a few minutes.

In her absence, Tad continued to look over their fine work. "The place looks much nicer, Jem. I don't see why people think this place is haunted. Even with the overgrowth and the darkness," he gestured at the shadows growing longer and thicker around them, "it doesn't seem that sinister."

Jemma couldn't agree more, but she shushed him as Mama B emerged with a paper bag. Whatever was in it smelled very good. *Or maybe I'm starving,* Jemma told herself.

Mama B handed the bag to Tad. "Some fresh bread and preserves."

Jemma's eyes widened. *Fresh? How could that be?* Mama B had been at her side all day, giving her no time to bake anything.

"Ah, thank you," Tad replied. "I can feel how warm it is. I haven't had fresh bread since..." His words trailed off as an unwanted memory came to mind. He forced a smile. "Anyway, thank you so much, ma'am. I mean, Mama B." He tapped his forehead. "I didn't forget."

The old woman smiled broadly. She turned to Jemma. "See you tomorrow, my dear." She turned and reentered her house.

The trip home was a lot better in her father's truck than on foot. As they passed the part of the road where she had first seen the teens of Solomon's Cross, she peered out, but the parking spots in front of the old tackle shack were empty. No one was there.

It wasn't until they got home that Jemma realized her backpack was lighter than it had been that morning. She looked inside and gasped. The photo album wasn't there. *What the hell did I do with it? I must have left it on the bench and not noticed it was still there when I gathered my things to leave.* Missing such a thing wasn't something Jemma normally did.

"Anything wrong, Jem?" Tad asked.

Jemma shook her head. "No, nothing's wrong." To herself, she added, *I'll get it tomorrow.*

The thought of the photo album's disappearance left her mind when Tad handed her the paper bag with the bread and preserves. "I don't like sweets much, Jem, you know that, but I think I'll enjoy this."

Jemma took the bag. Her father's smile was tired but genuine. Delilah loved to bake. At least, she had loved it when Jemma knew her well. The two of them had spent Saturday mornings making all kinds of baked goods, none of which her father liked because he was the opposite of a sweets guy. Despite that, both felt the bittersweetness of the memory.

Jemma hopped out of the car. "We'll split the loaf, but first, I need a shower."

CHAPTER SEVEN

The next few days passed by quickly, full of hard work and long days in the sun as autumn approached. Jemma alternated between working at Gran's Rest and spending the few mandatory hours a week necessary to keep up with her schoolwork. Both work and school were going well, so she had little time to think about the journal pages stowed in her closet. Since the first time she had tried transcribing what was written on them, she hadn't had another moment to look at them.

On her second day of work, Jemma found the photo album on the bench behind the house where she had left it, though she was certain it had been in her bag before she saw her father. Despite her immense and ever-growing curiosity about it and Mama B's connection to the house she now lived in, she forgot about it every time she worked. Each time she thought to bring it up, something distracted her. After a week of working there, the photo album had stayed on the stone bench, untouched.

Every day, Mama B worked beside Jemma, often doing

as much work as the younger woman and sometimes more. Jemma had shared a lot about her life on the first day, and gradually, Mama B began to talk about her own life as well.

"This place used to look so nice. So nice. So very nice," she murmured one afternoon as the sun beamed down upon them. Jemma couldn't always tell when the old woman was talking to her and when she was talking to herself. "We used to get all sorts of visitors coming through here. All kinds of people, we'd have. All kinds."

She never mentioned who "we" included, but it sounded like Mama B hadn't always been the only person living up here and running it. She couldn't imagine the woman running a bed and breakfast on her own.

Jemma dared ask a question at last. "Did you have a groundskeeper when all the people used to come here?"

Mama B nodded, a small smile pulling at her lips. A fond memory shone in her eyes. "Yes, a fine man used to keep the grounds." She winked at Jemma as she straightened, a bundle of freshly picked herbs resting in her lap. "So fine a groundskeeper he was, he soon became something else."

Jemma's brows rose, then she wiggled them. "A beau, perhaps?" she teased the old woman.

"Oh, hush, child," Mama B answered, chuckling. "He fought in the Second Great War over in France. He trained in the Colorado Rockies, mountains like the ones around us now." She gestured at the peaks within view. "Then he went to France and fought in the Alps. A brave man, he was, a very brave man."

Jemma's hands slowed. *Wait, the Second Great War?*

WWII had been over for seventy-five years or more. All Jemma had heard about Mrs. Brickellwood being old since residents of Solomon's Cross had been children came back to her. She also remembered the newspaper clippings and faded photographs in Harv's diner about World War II.

"What was his name?" she ventured.

Mama B turned, her eyes shining with nostalgia and happiness. "His name was Solomon, child."

Jemma's eyes widened. Was this town named after the man Mama B spoke of? She didn't think that was possible since the town had been around before the Second Great War.

She set her confusion aside and resumed the pace she had set earlier. She smiled. Jemma found she liked working with the old woman far more than she would ever have thought. Not only was she stimulating company, but she was also kind and gave helpful direction. Jemma felt like she was earning her wages and learning useful skills at the same time. She couldn't believe the people down the mountain thought she was a witch. She was a little strange sometimes, but nothing sinister.

Every time the memory of the kids her age in Solomon's Cross spreading rumors and names about Mrs. Brickellwood came to Jemma's mind, she got defensive.

There is another strange thing, though, Jemma added to herself the day Mama B told the story about the war veteran-turned-groundskeeper. She remembered how, on the first day she met the old woman, Mrs. Brickellwood told her everyone called her Mama B. Who was everyone? Certainly not the townspeople of Solomon's Cross. Certainly not the young people Jemma's age. And yet,

Mama B did not seem ignorant of the stories people told about her.

So, which is it? Jemma wondered. Did the old woman think she was a loving grandmother figure living on the side of a mountain or an elusive witch who ate any children who came to her? Mrs. Eloise Brickellwood's reputation, it seemed, was a contradictory, strange, and mysterious affair.

The longer I work here, Jemma decided, *the more likely I am to find out what's going on.*

Mrs. Eloise Brickellwood's reputation came up later that week when Jemma found time to spend the evening hanging with Easter and Val McCarthy at Harv's diner. The invitation had been extended by the siblings, and even though Jemma hadn't hung out with anyone her age for quite some time, she accepted it eagerly.

The two of them had come by Jemma's new house a time or two. "Just passin' by" or "Stoppin' for a jawin,'" which Jemma realized meant "a chat" were a couple of the excuses they used to visit with her. Tad was always delighted to have them over. Jemma got those chances to get to know them a little better, but they were short-lived. She was busy with work and school, and the McCarthys also had school as well as numerous, unending errands to run for their folks in Val's old beater of a truck, plus drives to Johnson City Hospital about twenty miles away for Easter's condition.

Two weeks after Jemma met the McCarthys, the stars

finally aligned. Easter and Val had an evening when they were free and Jemma didn't have homework. She also wasn't bone-tired from working at Gran's Rest since Mama B had sent her home halfway through the day. So, it only seemed natural that the three of them would share a meal.

Harv's had been Easter's suggestion, and although Jemma hadn't been keen on going there again, she found she liked it much better the second time around. Being with the regulars in a place they enjoyed being in made Harv's diner look different in Jemma's eyes. There was a warmth and coziness to the atmosphere that hadn't been there when it had just been Jemma and her father. The workers knew the McCarthys. Smiles and nods of greeting were shared. The same smiles were extended to Jemma. The people at Harv's seemed to be opening up to the idea of newcomers, even if it was just two of them.

Thanks to the generous paycheck Jemma received from her grounds and landscaping work, she and Val ordered everything on the menu that looked even halfway good: burgers, fries, grilled cheese sandwiches, three different flavors of milkshakes, pickles spears, and a root beer float to top it all off. The two of them devastated the food as only teens could. Easter, easily made nauseous, took her time and ate sparingly.

In the afterglow of so many consumed calories, their conversation shifted from gossip about town regulars in the diner to the topic of Jemma's employer. "I don't get it. Why does everyone have such a dark view of the old woman?" Jemma asked as she polished off a strawberry milkshake. She had told the two siblings time and time again about how gentle and kind Mrs. Brickellwood was. She was far from the child-eating witch portrayed in fairytales.

Easter and Val shared a long look across the table. Val sat next to Jemma so they could share the food, while Easter sat across from them. The McCarthys were Kalhoun natives. Their insight was invaluable to Jemma.

"Our parents have told us it wasn't always that way," Easter answered. She had leaned forward and lowered her voice. "At one time, everyone knew Mama B was strange, and they all called her that too, it's true. Some even joked about her being supernaturally strange, but no one would have ever called her a witch."

Val nodded. "Yeah, everyone seemed to get along with her fine and leave her alone. Nobody minded if visitors came to the county and stayed up on the mountain at her place."

"What changed, then?" Jemma pressed.

Easter shrugged. "Not sure. She used to come to town all the time to visit two friends of hers, both women, then one day, it stopped."

Jemma's brows furrowed together. "What other women?"

"Well," Easter continued, leaning forward on her elbows, "Mama B had two old friends, both women but neither of them as ancient-looking as she was. At least, that's what we've heard. Neither Val nor I ever saw them. Her two friends died when our parents were kids. That's when it changed, I think."

Val nodded again. "After her friends died, the old woman became withdrawn. She spent less time in town.

That's when the dark whispers and muttering grew up around her like weeds."

Jemma was more intrigued than ever. Her surroundings, other than the booth she sat in and her two companions, seemed to disappear. The glow of the diner shone around them, bathing them in yellow light as they conversed. Outside, night had fallen. "What were the names of her two friends?"

Val shrugged. "Beats me. Our parents don't even know."

"There was more to it, we've been told," Easter added. "There was some business having to do with a coal company that ain't around anymore and a dispute involving land Mrs. Brickellwood's husband owned."

Mama B hadn't mentioned a husband, and she didn't wear a wedding ring. The old woman hadn't mentioned any family. Jemma wondered if her husband had been Solomon, the war veteran-turned-groundskeeper.

"When was this?" Jemma asked, also wondering if the land dispute had anything to do with where her new home was built. It made sense since it was so close to where the old coal mining entrances were.

"Sometime before my parents were even born," Easter replied. "Whatever happened, we've all been raised to know there's something mysterious and strange about the woman." The girl shook her head. "But perhaps the sinister reputation is unfair." She gave Jemma a tired smile. "You've met her, and I believe what you say about her. Most people in this town haven't spoken a word to her. Not anyone our age, anyway."

Jemma remembered that all the patrons in this very diner had chimed in with their opinions on the old woman that first night when she and her father had brought the photo album inside. She leaned back, crossed her arms, and sighed. "Well, she is odd; I'll give them that. She says strange things now and then, but she's nice enough."

Val smirked. "And she pays well." He gestured at their now-empty plates and glasses and slurped the last of the melted ice cream from the bottom of the root beer float cup. Jemma had insisted on paying because even though she was too polite to say it, the McCarthys were poor, thanks to hospital bills and whatever else had befallen the family.

"What all are you doing up there anyway?" the teenage boy asked after finishing the drink.

Jemma explained the work and how, even though it sounded boring, she found it more fulfilling than she could have ever expected. "You wouldn't believe how much Mama B knows about herbs and plants and their medicinal uses. I didn't realize nature could be as healing as that." Jemma's eyes brightened as she explained. Biology and chemistry had always been her favorite subjects in school, so seeing them in her everyday life was rewarding.

"Ha. Maybe I should go to Mama B then instead of all the doctors that aren't doing one damn thing for me." Easter scoffed, half-joking. She chuckled, but Jemma had the sense that she was serious.

"Come on, Easter! They aren't that bad," Val interjected.

"But it's true," Easter protested without sounding bitter or angry. Jemma admired that, given the girl's long-standing condition. "They don't have one damn clue how to help me." She shrugged. "No one seems to have a clue.

Not one person. What's wrong with seeing if the old woman on the mountain knows something?"

Dozens of moments where Mama B had "known something" without Jemma telling her came to mind. It was sometimes disconcerting.

Val didn't respond, just stared at the table. This was the first time since meeting them that Easter had spoken so openly about her illness. Jemma saw it as an opportunity to learn more. "If you don't mind telling me, what is your illness?" she asked.

To her surprise, Val snapped his head up and looked in the direction opposite from Jemma: out the window into the street, which would have been pitch-black if it weren't for the glow of a streetlight. The sound he made was suspiciously similar to the sniffles Jemma's father gave out when he was trying to keep his emotions in check.

Easter shook her head at her brother's reaction, then shrugged in defeat. "We don't know. Some doctors think it's an autoimmune disease where my body sickens from attacking itself. Other doctors think it's from environmental contagion, but none of them can identify it, and no one else seems to have the same illness."

Jemma listened intently. An ache bloomed in her chest and spread throughout her body. Her heart reached out to her newfound friend. Paired with this compassion was the sense of helplessness she had often felt when faced with her father's depression. Oftentimes, Jemma felt like she only knew how to stand and watch. She didn't know how to help.

"It started years ago," Easter continued as her brother

kept staring out the window into the darkness, "but it has steadily gotten worse."

Finally, Val turned from the window and spoke in his cracking, quavering voice. "We'll figure it out." He gave the girls an earnest look. Jemma recognized the fear in his eyes, fear of having someone close to him lose themselves to an inner sickness and not being able to do a damn thing about it. "You'll get better. We don't need to talk about it anymore," Val finished.

That was it. End of discussion.

A flash of big-sister irritation in Easter's eyes did not escape Jemma's notice. After looking at Val's face for a long moment, however, Easter relented. She nodded. "We shouldn't talk about it anymore." She looked at Jemma. "Especially since our new friend won't want to spend all her time with a pair of sad saps."

Jemma gave them a reassuring smile. "There is no one else in this town I'd rather spend my time with." Relief came into Easter's and Val's expressions. Jemma had the feeling Easter's illness was only the surface of what the McCarthy family was going through. She didn't want to push, though.

I want to help, she thought. Her heart went out to these two seemingly lonely kids. Perhaps all they had gone through was why she had never heard them mention other friends or kids from school. They spoke with disdain about AJ Kilmer sometimes but made no mention of the other kids they had been with the night Jemma met them.

Jemma would ask Mama B what she might be able to do for Easter. She decided not to let the girl or Val know she was going to do that. The conversation about her sickness was over, and Jemma didn't want to give her false hope in case the old woman couldn't help.

It was worth a try.

After Jemma paid the bill, the three left the diner and stepped into the warm late-summer night. In a couple of weeks, the nights would be significantly cooler. The truck was parked in front of the diner, but Jemma's attention was drawn to the commotion beyond it. Across the street, against the front of a store, stood a group of people around her age. There were five or six, some of them smoking but all of them talking in low voices with the occasional laugh.

"Wait, I recognize them," Jemma blurted before she thought to keep her words in.

At the sound of Val's truck door opening, eyes turned in their direction. Jemma recognized the girl with the purple streak in her hair. The girl smiled at the three, whom she seemed to recognize—even Jemma, to whom she hadn't been introduced. She waved before turning back to her companions. Others cast glances their way without acknowledging them.

"What's up with them?" she muttered.

Easter climbed into the passenger seat and closed the door without a second look in the direction of her peers. Val paused before the driver's side door. He didn't open it yet. "The kids around here are weird about us. Sometimes they're all friendly and inviting and shit. Sometimes it's like we're invisible."

Jemma shrugged. It didn't matter to her. She had two new friends, and that was more than she'd thought she'd have for the first year after moving here.

She reached to open the back door, but Val put a hand

on her arm, stopping her. She turned to find him wearing a tired yet earnest smile. "Thank you for being our friend, Jemma. I know it's just started, but I need you to know that Easter hasn't been this happy in a long time. You make her happy. That's a very good thing."

Jemma smiled in return. "I hope I can be a good friend to her and to you. I'm glad to have *you* as a friend as well."

Val grinned and nodded before he opened the door and got in. They headed out so Val could drop Jemma off at her house. Jemma waved goodbye as they drove off. Easter smiled at her from the open window.

Tomorrow morning, Jemma promised, she would ask the old woman on the mountain if she could do anything to help her friend. The doctors in Johnson City might not have been doing Easter McCarthy any good, but the so-called witch on the mountain and her plants, Jemma was certain, could.

CHAPTER EIGHT

During the first couple of weeks working at Gran's Rest, Jemma and Mama B had mostly cleared the grounds except for the tiered slope at the back where the outdoor cooking and entertaining used to happen.

Fall was setting in. The hot days were no more. The end of September brought about a gradual change in color around them. The grass was less green. Half the leaves on the trees weren't green anymore. Since autumn was almost upon them, the last of the herb and late-year mushroom crop needed to be harvested, according to Mama B.

Therefore, the day would be spent gathering herbs, mushrooms, and any other plants the old woman deemed necessary to "survive the winter." This perplexed Jemma at first, but then she remembered that Mama B never went into town anymore. Anything she needed to survive, she procured from her grounds. So, for her sake, Jemma set to work.

They gathered the mushrooms using Mama B's method of pulling them upward while twisting them in a counterclockwise direction. Carefully, she added, so that the mycelium would not be broken. As they did that, the old woman prattled on about the old days when they had regular visitors. Mama B never mentioned the same people twice. The groundskeeper, Solomon, hadn't been brought up again since the old woman's first mention of him.

Once more, Jemma couldn't quite figure out how much of Mama B's talking was for her. The old woman always seemed to be muttering something under her breath.

Today, however, she spoke in a clear voice so Jemma could hear every word.

"We had regulars every day, even if they weren't staying the night. Many would come up for breakfast." Mama B shook her head and chuckled. "Diners in town hated me. Took all their business up the mountain!"

Jemma thought of Harv's diner and wondered if it had been around during the time Mama B was referring to. She then wondered if some of the visitors who came to Gran's Rest every day were the two women who had been her friends.

Perhaps Mama B had guessed what was on Jemma's mind. It wasn't beyond the realm of possibility. "I had two friends. Dear, dear friends." Her tone was wistful, and she looked into the distance as if the faces of her friends were painted on the sides of the mountain.

Jemma listened intently. "Did they come to visit you here?"

"Yes and no," Mama B answered. "They helped me run the place for some time, but then, after getting married and so on, they moved into the town." Her expression darkened. "Their husbands didn't want them up here on the mountain all the time."

"Sounds like a lovely turn of events," Jemma answered dryly.

The old woman sighed as she plopped a newly picked mushroom onto the apron draped over her lap, "It is what it is."

"What were your friends' names?" Jemma ventured.

Mama B didn't seem to hear her, or perhaps she ignored the question. "We were closer than sisters, the three of us." She looked toward the mountain again, speaking in the same wistful tone as before. "One dead and one gone."

Jemma's brow creased in confusion and curiosity. What did she mean by that? How had the one died, and where had the other gone? She wanted to ask, but the old woman had moved on.

"There were many very interesting visitors to Gran's Rest. Once, a man older than I who played the bagpipes came. Every day, like the rooster who crows, he would stand on the top of the hill and play a morning tune. We liked it at first, but gradually, everyone got tired of it. He stayed for weeks, doing the same thing every morning." She laughed. "He only knew one damn song."

She continued to prattle, but Jemma did not listen. She was stuck on Mama B's words: "Older than I." She imagined the old woman had once been young, though the confusion in town about her age still played through her mind. Perhaps the rumors were baseless and born of fear. The people didn't understand her. Therefore, they decided they were afraid of her.

I'm not, Jemma thought.

Mama B continued describing guests who had come to the top of the mountain, seeking help for their illnesses. Some had come to spend the last weeks of their lives in this picturesque place, only to find that with the help of the owner, they could live a little longer. Still others had come for fresh mountain air to cure their lungs and were given more. Many left Gran's Rest in better physical condition than they had arrived in.

"You helped a lot of people," Jemma remarked.

Mama B turned to her with a smile pulling at the corners of her mouth and nodded. "I suppose I did. Sometimes it was relief from medicinal herbs." She pointed at the pile of mushrooms they had pulled and winked at Jemma. "Other times, it was just advice."

The old woman's eyes turned toward the house, and a sad expression came over her face. Jemma looked in the same direction. She hadn't been inside the house once. It wasn't that the old woman told her she couldn't, but even when Jemma needed to use the bathroom, Mama B directed her to an outhouse instead of letting her inside. They ate their lunches on the porch, never indoors.

She wondered what it was like inside. Was it in as much disarray as the grounds had been weeks ago? What would happen when winter came? They would not be able to work on the grounds. It would be too cold. Would the old woman let her come into the house?

Mama B's voice broke through Jemma's thoughts. "Once, a whole group of children in the house came down with chickenpox. They were here for weeks but were better about halfway through their time. They just wanted to stay on."

The mention of children made Jemma remember the photo album. "Yes, I remember seeing pictures of you with what looked like children and grandchildren around you in the photo album." In the photos, Mama B had looked much younger. "Who were they? Do you have a family?"

Jemma hoped to God the old woman would give her direct answers this time.

Mama B slowed in her labors for the first time and looked into the distance instead of at the young woman beside her. "No, dearie, those weren't my young 'uns." She nodded as a memory came over her. "They were children I helped bring into the world, though." She turned slightly, now looking at Jemma. There was a distant sadness in her eyes. "I was a midwife many years ago. I brought dozens of babies into this world and saved those lives later on with the very things we're pulling from the ground now." She smiled fondly. "They weren't my children, but they might as well have been. I gave them advice, they went and roamed the world, and then they came back and told me all about their adventures."

"And then what?" Jemma asked breathlessly.

"Well, then they died," Mama B said as if the answer was obvious. "Some from old age, others from sicknesses I couldn't be there to cure."

Jemma's brows furrowed. How could it be that Mama B had brought someone into the world and was still around when they died of old age? This question faded in as Easter's face popped into her mind. "I have a friend who is sick, Mama B. She says all the doctors in Johnson City can't help her. They don't know what's wrong with her. Maybe you could help."

"Tell me about her."

Jemma explained Easter's symptoms. Mama B inquired about her appearance, and Jemma answered as best she could.

"How long has this been going on?" the old woman asked.

"I don't know exactly." Jemma rubbed at a spot of dirt on her forehead. "A long time, though."

Concern deepened the wrinkles on Mama B's face. "Tell me what she's like."

Jemma wasn't sure what Easter's personality had to do with her condition, but she obliged the old woman. "She's kind but fierce. She has a younger brother she loves. Dry sense of humor." Jemma smiled, remembering the fun the three of them had already had in such a short time after her move here. If only Easter felt better when they spent time together. They could get into all sorts of mischief.

When Jemma finished, Mama B nodded, stood, and shuffled into the house through the back door. She reappeared moments later with a glass container in hand. "Paste of pilewort, skull cap, and grindle sprout," she explained.

Thanks to Jemma's work over the past few weeks, she had heard of these ingredients. She took the container from Mama B's extended hand. The old woman explained how it should be used. "Tell your friend to rub it on her chest, stomach, and temples. It should help with the nausea and fatigue and improve her appetite. It's not a cure, but it should help some." The old woman produced a kind smile.

"Thank you," Jemma replied. "You have no idea how grateful I am."

The old woman chuckled. "Maybe I do, dearie. Friendship is valuable; that I know well. We must take care of those dear to us."

They came to a good stopping place at the end of the path and went to the porch for lunch. Jemma wasn't sure when Mama B had had time to bake a loaf of fresh bread and make preserves, but both were in place when they got there. There were also apple cider and thick slices of cheese.

Jemma wolfed the food down. After they finished, they sat back in their rocking chairs, which were side by side, and enjoyed the warmth of the afternoon. The day was particularly sunny and warm for late September. It was so comfortable that, in almost no time, the old woman had dozed off.

Jemma thought about taking a nap too, but another idea came to her. If Mama B was asleep, she wouldn't see Jemma going into the house. *Oh, shut up,* she told herself. *You're not going to sneak around like that, especially while she's asleep.*

Then she realized there wouldn't be another opportunity as good as that moment. Jemma stole a glance at the old woman. She was still asleep. Sneaking around her employer's property wasn't anything Jemma would even think to do normally, but the idea kept pulling at her. She wanted to know what was inside. *If I go in for just a second, she won't even know,* she decided. *And she never told me I couldn't.* Still, it felt like she was doing something wrong.

Before Jemma could convince herself that it was a very

bad idea, she had gotten to her feet and was walking toward the front door. She eased it open slowly, watching the sleeping woman all the while. She slipped inside and closed the door behind her.

The interior of the house was dim, lit only by the sunlight filtering through stained curtains hanging from rods over the windows. Everything seemed to be covered in a layer of dust. Cobweb-laden sofas and chairs littered a parlor and a den. The dining room held a mismatched conglomeration of chipped dining chairs and a wobbling table upon which was set a lazy Susan with an oil lamp in desperate need of a wash. The lace tablecloth was yellowed and stiff. Dishes were piled high in the kitchen sink.

Jemma stopped in the doorway between the dining room and the kitchen. In the hall beyond was a staircase leading to the second floor, where she assumed the bedrooms were. True to her expectations, the inside of the house was in disarray. It did not, however, seem the kind of disorder that would come about as a result of a little old lady having no one to help her. It appeared this way because Mama B hadn't had the will to make it look like it once was. Perhaps the people who had grown afraid of her refused to come here.

"She became an outcast," Jemma murmured. "Unwanted. Alone." She rubbed her arms. It was cold in here. She much preferred the sunshine outside. Something else, however, kept her rooted to the spot. At first glance, the interior of the house looked unkempt but held ordinary contents. When she looked again, Jemma saw things she wouldn't have expected to be inside the house.

Photographs and paintings of people covered the walls.

Some were crooked or dangled from a nail. All had one thing in common; the eyes of the people in the pictures were covered with black paint. A long line of black ran over the eyes so Jemma could not see the portraits staring at her. She shuddered. It was very strange, and she didn't like it one bit.

Further, there were dozens of teapots in the kitchen and dining room but no teacups or saucers. Pieces of parchment with tight, cramped writing were scattered about these two rooms as well. Jemma wondered what she would find if she looked at the parlor and den again. What would she see in the hall? She had spied a great grandfather clock and crept into the hall to take a closer look. The clock was ticking but off by at least four hours.

Jemma got the sense that being in here was a bad idea. First, she had snuck inside while Mama B was asleep, breaking her trust. Second, the place was eerie. She shuddered again. The contents of the house were by no means sinister, but they were strange and out of place. What did the condition and contents of the house say about the woman who lived in it? Many unkind descriptions came to Jemma's mind, all things she had heard from the people in Solomon's Cross.

No, it's not like that. It's your imagination, Jemma told herself, wanting more than anything to believe Mama B wasn't the witch those in town rumored her to be.

Jemma snapped out of her thoughts when she heard feet shuffling over the floorboards. She whirled, heart thundering, to see a figure emerge from the parlor. Mama B looked at Jemma with disappointed eyes. They stared at one another in tense silence.

Shit! She woke up and saw me gone! And then, *Wait, how did she get in here? I didn't hear the door open.* She glanced at the front door and then at the back door at the other end. Both doors were shut, and she doubted the old woman had climbed through a window, so how did she do it? Jemma was growing more uncomfortable by the second, and now there was the added layer of being caught.

"We were supposed to be able to trust one another," the old woman murmured. She didn't sound angry but rather deeply disappointed.

Jemma's heart sank. *I fucked this one up.* For a fleeting moment, she wondered if she had lost her job. It would be devastating if she had since the work at Gran's Rest had become far more than a job to her.

"Go on home now, dearie. I think it is best to leave me alone for a time," Mama B added. She led Jemma to the door and closed it behind her once she was on the porch. Jemma stood still for a long moment in shock. She turned back, thinking she could knock on the door and sort this out with her employer. The door, however, had closed with a sense of finality. She had no choice but to go home.

Jemma gathered her things: the backpack with the photo album inside and the paste Mama B had given her for Easter.

She felt sick to her stomach as she left.

I've broken her trust, she thought. *I messed up.*

Those thoughts followed Jemma down the mountain and along the paved road until she reached her gravel drive.

She stood for a moment in the front yard, wondering who had lived in her house before. Many times, she had thought to ask Mama B about her connection to the home, but now it seemed like she would never get the answer.

She dismissed her thoughts of the old woman for the time being and turned to thinking about Easter. She still had the paste, and she hoped to God it would help her friend. Now that she had better cell phone service, she called the McCarthy siblings. "Come by when you can. I have something that could help Easter."

They arrived after school was let out. Val was driving, of course. Tad wasn't home yet, so the three had the house to themselves. "Mama B gave it to me." She explained to Easter how to use it and how it would help her.

Easter's eyes filled with light. "Thank you so much, Jemma. I'm sure it'll help some even if it's not a cure."

"My thoughts exactly," Jemma replied.

Val, however, didn't seem as sure. His eyes flashed as he looked at Jemma. "You shouldn't be going to a witch to talk about my sister."

Taken aback, Jemma's eyes widened. "I was trying to help—"

Her words were cut off as Easter turned on her brother. "Come on, Val, don't talk shit. You know Mom and Dad wouldn't want to hear you speaking about Mama B like that, especially since she was kind enough to try to help me."

Val crossed his arms and muttered under his breath, "It's probably seasoning for when Mama B comes to eat you."

Anger flashed in Easter's eyes. "If it helps me not feel so

damn awful all the time, then I'll gladly use it, seasoning or no. It'll be a damn sight better than the drugs those doctors force down my throat or into my veins. I'm a shell of a person, Val! Maybe this will make me less like that. And for God's sake, you sound like AJ right now."

Jemma stood back, shocked by the volatility in the siblings' interaction. She had never seen them argue with one another. However, she knew siblings could be like that sometimes. As an only child, she had never experienced it.

Easter's rebuke quieted Val. He stared at the floor for a long time before murmuring a dismal, "I'm sorry, Easter."

Jemma laid a comforting hand on Easter's arm. "If it works, I can get plenty more." As she said that, however, she wasn't certain she could. Jemma Nox wasn't sure the so-called witch on the mountain would have her back.

Later, as she went up the ladder into the loft, she thought about all the pictures hanging in Mama B's house. "All those painted-out eyes." She shook her head, still wondering about it as she got ready for bed.

CHAPTER NINE

"No work today?" Tad asked Jemma the next morning when he found her eating breakfast alone in the kitchen.

I think it's best to leave me alone for a time, played in Jemma's mind. What had Mama B meant by "a time?" She forced a smile as she turned to her father. "Eggs?"

Tad waved in dismissal. "I've already eaten." He leaned against the counter and waited for her answer.

"Not today," Jemma told him with a sigh she could not contain. "She told me to take a couple of days off and focus on school."

Tad's brows knitted. "Are you having trouble with school, Jem?"

Jemma shook her head, deciding she would tell him part of the truth. She wasn't ready to tell her father what she had seen inside Mama B's house. The images of those paintings with the eyes painted out had stained her dreams, and she still thought about them now that she was awake.

"Well then," Tad announced with his broadest smile and

most cheerful voice, "I'll take a day off too!" He scanned the kitchen. "I'm thinking there are some things we could fix up around here. What do you say about going into town for supplies so we can do touch-ups around the house?"

Jemma's brows rose. "Did you decide not to have the handyman come back?"

Tad nodded. "Whatever he can fix, I can too!" Jemma frowned, and Tad laughed. "You doubt my manly around-the-house skills."

"And for good reason," Jemma responded with her mouth full. She downed a glass of orange juice, then added, "We can go when I'm done with homework. How does that sound?"

Hours later, they pulled out of the gravel driveway and made their way down the rest of the mountain. The diner, small bank, car repair shop, general store, and gas station were right there when they entered the town, about three miles from their house. Tad pulled the truck into a parking space at RJ's Lumber and Tools. The place was one of the last at which Jemma had tried to get a job before the lady at the desk gave her a look that said, "We only hire people we know, and we don't know you." After that, Jemma had given up.

She followed her father inside anyway. Tad took his time, as he was accustomed to doing, so Jemma wandered away. She was more interested in looking at paint than repair items. *Maybe I can paint the loft a lighter color so it doesn't look so dingy*, she thought.

Jemma was trying to decide between Canyon Iris and Indigo Batik when voices behind her diverted her attention. She turned to see two young men standing by the counter. One of them she didn't recognize, but the other was AJ Kilmer.

Her fists involuntarily clenched at her sides.

"Put the damn cigarette out before your father sees ya," a black-haired youth in a white tank top and jeans hissed at his friend.

AJ sighed, rolled his eyes, and put the cigarette out with such a dramatic air that Jemma also rolled her eyes. He looked over his shoulder at an older man in the back office.

Jemma's eyes widened. AJ Kilmer's father owned this shop. Ronald Jean was his name. How Tad had found out before he told Jemma on the way here, she did not know. What she did know was that Ronald Jean had a son, and he was Jemma's least favorite person in Solomon's Cross so far.

Before she could turn away so AJ wouldn't see her, his sharp eyes drifted past his friend and the shelves lined with cans of paint and met hers. Recognition filled his face. His lips curled back. He bared his teeth and hissed. His friend glanced back and frowned, confused. AJ muttered something to him, and although Jemma didn't hear his words, she knew they were about her.

He was pissed at her for being here. She muttered, "Shit," under her breath. "Of course. The one time I come into town, expecting not to see him."

He sauntered over in his lithe, catlike manner, eyes flashing. A threat was on the tip of his tongue. It was only a matter of time before it slid off. Jemma stood motionless, unable to move for whatever goddamn reason. She could hear her father prattling to someone he probably just met two aisles over in the small store. AJ stopped in front of her. She could smell cigarette smoke on him. It wouldn't matter if his father saw him smoking or not. He would know. AJ wore the same oil-stained clothes he'd been in when she'd first met him.

He smirked. "Hey there, witch slave. Glad to find you here."

"My name is Jemma," she replied. "You don't have to call me anything. In fact, you don't need to speak a single word to me."

AJ chuckled as Jemma turned away. "Slow down, why don't you? We never got properly introduced."

Something made her turn back, although her brain screamed, "Don't waste a fucking second of your time on this guy!"

He extended a dirty hand. "Name's AJ Kilmer."

Jemma stared at his hand until he dropped it.

AJ sighed. "And you're Jemma Nox. You didn't need to tell me your name."

"Why the hell did you think we should introduce ourselves if you already knew my name?" she snapped.

AJ shrugged, his smirk growing larger. He was getting what he wanted: a reaction. "I figured you needed to know *my* name."

His name was the last thing Jemma needed to know, but she answered, "I already knew."

"Whatever, witch slave," AJ replied. He leaned against a shelf with paint on it and crossed his arms. "You know my old man runs this store, right?"

Jemma had guessed as much. "Yeah. Sounds like he'd be pissed if he found you smoking in it."

AJ's expression darkened, but his sinister smile

widened. "Spying on me, eh? You know, I could have you thrown out of here for consorting with a witch. Wouldn't want any curses cast on my old man's shop. He needs the money."

Jemma frowned. She remembered seeing AJ's sleek sportscar. Only a wealthy family could afford that.

Jemma thought of dozens of heated retorts, but she settled for a cool, nonchalant response. She looked at her fingernails as if they were far more interesting than anything AJ had to say. "No curses today, but I do wonder if your head is okay after that knock on the concrete." She glanced up and shrugged. AJ looked like he was going to explode. She lit the match and set it to the bomb's fuse. "I can see if Mama B can brew something up for you to help with headaches."

The bomb went off. The reminder of AJ's humiliation enraged him. The next instant, he was in her face. His cheeks flamed red. His eyes flashed with anger. When he spoke, his saliva spattered her face. "If you feel so tough, witch slave, why don't you hit me again? I don't think you will. My back ain't turned this time."

Jemma wondered if he always threatened girls. How many street fights had he engaged in? Since they were in a public place, she hadn't seen him as a threat. However, she spat back, "Maybe you should get out of my way and get back to stocking shelves."

AJ snarled, and before Jemma knew what was happening, he had put both his hands on her shoulders and shoved her into a shelf of paint. She hit it with enough force to bring down a few cans. They exploded on the floor, spattering her clothes.

The commotion signaled others in the store. A second later, Tad Nox came around the corner, looking concerned. Concern morphed into surprise and then indignation. Tad realized what was going on right away. Jemma didn't say a word about who AJ was, but Tad knew. He was in AJ's face before anyone could stop him. Jemma had never seen him so angry. He grabbed the young man by the front of his shirt and jerked him forward. "I'll turn you inside out if you ever touch my daughter again." Then he released AJ, who staggered back.

AJ looked more surprised than hurt. He hadn't hit the shelf like Jemma. He gathered himself and straightened to his full height. He was a head taller than Jemma's father, but Tad didn't seem to notice. "Hitting people from behind is the only thing you and your daughter know how to do!" He stepped forward, fists clenched like he was going to fight Tad, too.

Jemma couldn't believe it. This was the last thing she had expected to happen as a result of a trip to town.

Tad put out a hand to stop AJ. The young man stared at it and sneered. Tad continued, "Take another step toward me or my daughter, and you'll be scooping up your shattered teeth with broken fingers." Jemma believed Tad could do it. So did AJ. He didn't back off right away, though. Conflict flickered in his eyes. Although she didn't like AJ Kilmer, she didn't want to see his teeth on the floor of his father's hardware store.

Before AJ could decide, a fourth person arrived on the scene. RJ Kilmer was a large, hulking man whose massive frame AJ pretended he was growing into. He'd gotten his height from his father but not the mass. Jemma shrank back. How was the owner going to react? RJ scanned the scene: the exploded paint cans, the mess on Jemma's clothes, the red-faced father standing beside his daughter, and finally, his son.

When he spoke, Jemma was surprised his voice was gentle and kind. "I'm sorry about all this." He turned to his son, and his face and voice grew stern. "Apologize immediately, AJ." AJ didn't have time to utter a word before RJ turned back to Tad and Jemma. "I am so sorry. So very sorry about this."

Tad's expression softened. "It's all right." He glared at AJ, waiting for his apology.

"Sorry," AJ mumbled, then got away as fast as he could. Jemma heard the bell on the front door tinkle as he opened it. The door slammed shut, and he was gone. She released a breath of relief.

RJ stooped to pick up the fallen paint cans. "AJ's been acting out more than ever lately. Not that that's an excuse, but I've asked those in town to bear with me as I figure out what to do about him."

Tad bent to help the distressed father. "Don't worry about us. It happens."

It should happen a lot less, Jemma thought as she gave her paint-spattered clothes a rueful look. Paint was difficult to get out of cloth. She wasn't looking forward to trying. She was, however, relieved that her father hadn't punched a minor. The police hadn't been called either, thankfully.

RJ shook his head. "I don't get it. I raised three daughters. They gave me a little bit of hell when they were in high school, but not as much as their baby brother."

"You have other children?" Tad asked. His normal

friendly personality came back. He spoke to RJ as if he expected them to become best friends.

RJ nodded. "Three daughters. All of them have moved out of Kalhoun County to pursue dreams or get married." He shook his head again. "But AJ? Well, he's different."

"I hope your wife is able to help you," Tad offered in an encouraging voice.

Sadness crept into RJ's expression. "My wife died three years ago. It's been me and AJ since then."

"I'm sorry for your loss," Tad told the man automatically. Jemma nodded. Although she disliked AJ, she already liked his father.

"Well, thank you," RJ answered. "AJ was troublesome before she died, and it got worse after she left us. He loved his mother dearly even when he acted like he didn't." The hulking man looked down as he fidgeted with the exploded paint can he had picked up. At last, he looked at Tad and then at Jemma. "I promise you I'll make sure my son never bothers either of you ever again. If you ever want to come to the store, I'll even send AJ to the back so you don't have to see him."

That seemed unnecessary. She could stay out of his way on her own. The owner of the store made his way to the front. Tad and Jemma followed. Tad laid the tools he wanted to purchase on the counter. Jemma, however, had not chosen a paint color.

"Another day," she muttered.

"On the house," RJ told Tad as the younger man pulled out his wallet.

"No, let me pay—" Tad started, but RJ waved a hand to dismiss his objection.

"It's the least I can do."

Tad gave his new friend a warm smile. "Well, thank you very much." A moment later, he and Jemma stepped out of the store into the warm autumn sunlight. Jemma spotted two other people she recognized standing by her father's truck. She smiled at Easter and Val McCarthy, who she was much happier to see than AJ Kilmer.

"We saw AJ storm out of here. I swear there was a big dark cloud over his head," Val remarked to Jemma. He scanned her paint-spattered clothes. "I'm guessing you might know why."

Jemma sighed. "A story for later. I don't think he's going to bother me anymore." She turned to Easter. "You're beaming today." It was true. Easter smiled like the sun.

"The paste you gave me has made a world of difference!" She gripped Jemma's arm excitedly. "Do you think Mama B has more?"

Val coughed and muttered something under his breath, but neither Jemma nor Easter paid him any mind.

"I think so," Jemma replied.

"Eee! Thank you!" Easter squealed. With more energy than Jemma had ever seen her exert, Easter flung her arms around her friend's neck. When she pulled back, she added, "I haven't told my parents yet. I don't want to give them any false hope, but I do feel better."

Relief flooded through Jemma. "I'm glad I could help you." Her heart sank the next moment, though, when she remembered Mama B didn't want her at Gran's Rest for an undetermined amount of time. She'd have to go up there and hope Mama B would accept her apology.

Her worry must have shown on her face since Easter asked, "Everything all right, Jemma?"

Jemma nodded and forced a smile. "I'll get you more as soon as I can."

Easter waved as Jemma got in the truck and Tad pulled out of town.

CHAPTER TEN

"Looks like you won't be going to work today," Tad remarked as he peered out the window. The sky was heavy with dark clouds, and the wind tore at the trees. A much-needed rain was coming soon. Tad stood between the window overlooking the porch and the front door, wearing business casual attire and holding a briefcase and an overnight bag.

"I'll be okay here by myself," Jemma told him. She gave him a reassuring smile. "Don't worry about me. Focus on your work, and when you get back in a few days, we can go have dinner at Harv's, and you can tell me all about it."

Tad's brows rose. "I thought you hated that diner."

Jemma smiled and shrugged. "Not as much as I hate eating boxed pizzas every night."

Tad frowned. "You only say that when I make them." Jemma didn't deny it. He sighed. "I'm a little worried about that AJ Kilmer kid coming around looking for trouble, and if I'm not here—"

"I'll punch him like I did the first time, Dad," Jemma

interrupted with a teasing smile. "Seriously, I'm going to be okay."

"Lock the door, please?" Tad requested as he opened it and stepped outside. He wanted to get to his truck before it started raining.

"Yes, I'll lock the door." Jemma laughed and rolled her eyes. "Though I think you're being ridiculous, letting a dumb kid get under your skin."

Tad put up his hands in defense. "*You* punched him, not me."

Jemma glowered at her father. "You almost did, and let us not forget the colorful threats you made."

Tad saluted her. "Trust me; they're not forgotten."

Jemma had to push her father out the door to get him to go. After a distant crack of thunder and another reassuring remark from Jemma, he went to his truck. Heavy drops pelted Jemma as she watched her father pull out of the drive. She turned and went into the house. She seldom had the place to herself. She thought about asking Easter and Val to come over, but it was midmorning. They were in school.

She had to find something to do on her own. She hadn't thought about the journals stowed in her closet until that moment. It was the perfect time. She didn't have work or school to do, and her father was away. "Time for a trip down the rabbit hole," she murmured as she climbed the ladder to the loft.

The first thing Jemma did was try to put the journal pages in chronological order. Since they had come loose from their binding, they were mixed up and scattered. The dates, however, were difficult to distinguish and ranged from World War II to ten years ago. The 1940s to 2011 was an odd span. It looked like all the pages were written by the same person. It was possible, but somehow, the pages from 2011 looked just as old as the pages from the 1940s—worn and ancient.

After she had sorted them as best as she could, she began to read and copy words she didn't recognize. The account she had already transcribed relayed that whoever the writer was, they had come to America from somewhere in Eastern Europe, traveled into the Appalachian Mountains, and was an herbal expert.

"Like Mama B," Jemma murmured, peering closely at one of the pages. She wondered if the old woman at Gran's Rest knew about the journal like she knew about the photo album. Jemma recognized some of the sketches of plants, thanks to Mama B's tutelage. The explanations for the herbs, however, were more about driving off evil spirits and supernatural-sounding creatures than treating headaches and fevers. Jemma found a list of words she didn't recognize.

Jinn
Kachina
Putti
Nocnica

On the next page was a list of words she did recognize.

Goblins
Ghouls
Gremlins

"They're all supernatural creatures," Jemma realized. Her eyes widened. This wasn't just some helpful medicinal information. This was written by someone who believed such creatures existed. "So, I'm dealing with a crazy person," she muttered. She was glad her father wasn't home to hear her. *She* sounded crazy.

Jemma turned to the next page. Here, the writing was crammed more than it normally was. She bent closer, trying to make out the words. Her eyes widened the longer she read on.

> *I encountered a young woman today who is afflicted with an illness I have not seen in many years. Her symptoms are consistent. She is weary after simple tasks. She is nauseous when she wakes and when she lays down to rest. She has fitful sleep, and she wishes to sleep every hour. Her skin is quite pale, paler than it's ever been, she told me. She hangs her head like someone on her way to a funeral. Sometimes, when I look into her eyes, I see nothing but her impending death. Nothing, she says, has been able to help. No doctors can find a way to help her. She thinks she has drunk contaminated water or that it is a result of a family illness. I do not see either of these to be the case.*

Jemma's eyes widened. Her heart hammered. The symptoms she was reading about sounded much like Easter's. She raced to the next line.

> *I believe she is being afflicted by a Nocnica.*

Jemma stopped for a moment. "Nocnica," she echoed. "That was in the list of creatures on the other page!"

Nocnica means "night woman." The locals would call her a boo hag. This is how she works her strange and bitter magic: She will hover above her sleeping victim and suck in his or her breath until she is full and can enter her victim. She will stay in the victim's skin as long as she can, wearing it as one would wear a cloak.

Jemma's fingers gripped the paper tighter. She was enthralled and terrified in equal measure.

A Nocnica is recognized by her translucent red figure, but they are difficult to see since they can make themselves small. So small as to slide through cracks and crevices. At night, their red coloring blends with the darkness, making them more difficult to distinguish.

Jemma shuddered. She could not take her eyes off the page. Suddenly, it wasn't as hard to distinguish the words.

I have found a way to keep the Night Woman away.

"Thank God," Jemma murmured. The writer instructed that an aromatic rub of dill and jewelweed be composed, which would keep the Night Woman from sucking the breath out of the victim and act as a deterrent.

The Night Woman is persistent. She will keep coming back. It is better to use the rub and then hunt down the creature, either kill it or drive it off. It can only be killed by

The rest of the page was blurred by water damage.

"Fuck!" Jemma hissed. She searched the other pages and found sketches of the herbs mentioned by the writer, as well as drawings of dill and jewelweed. *At least I know what they look like,* she thought.

Her heart rate increased. "I have to make this." An hour ago, she'd thought the writer of these journal entries was crazy for believing in supernatural creatures, but then she'd read about the very symptoms Easter suffered from.

"The doctors can't help her since her affliction is abnormal," Jemma concluded. She shook her head. "This is insane. There's no such thing as a Night Woman that sucks the breath from people while they sleep and then wears their skin." It sounded crazy. Still, what Jemma had read stuck with her. She couldn't get it out of her mind.

"Let's treat this whole thing like a science experiment. Like chemistry," she decided. She put the journals away. She didn't know how stiff she had become until she stood up. Jemma continued to think out loud. "It won't hurt to get the herbs I need and try to make it. If it doesn't do anything for Easter, then no harm done." The only problem was, Jemma didn't know if Mama B would trust her enough now to help her. The ingredients she needed were at Gran's Rest.

What happened if it did work? She swallowed hard, remembering what was written in the journal. If she found out Easter was being afflicted by a skin-wearing red monster, she would have to follow all the instructions. She'd have to hunt the damn thing down and kill it.

Jemma took a deep breath. "I'll cross that bridge when I get to it."

CHAPTER ELEVEN

Jemma had one day left before her father came home from his work trip. That meant she only had one day to experiment with the brew for Easter without him wondering what the hell she was concocting in their kitchen. She couldn't imagine him being happy about her mixing herbal remedies to drive off boo hags at any time or place, much less in his home.

She would have to go back to Gran's Rest if she wanted to help her friend. She didn't have a choice. She dreaded facing Mama B.

But I don't want to lose my job or my friend, she thought as she dressed and prepared herself for a hike to Gran's Rest.

At long last, the rain let up long enough for Jemma to trudge up the mountain. She had forgotten how long a trip it was since her father had been driving her there. The air was colder now that it was early October. The trees were bright with reds and oranges. The leaves covered the path as well. She wondered what the grounds would look like at Gran's Rest.

When Jemma arrived, she found that no work had been done since she was last here. That made sense. Even though Mama B could keep up with her, she wouldn't have been able to do any of it on her own. She stepped onto the porch, prepared with an apology, but she did not find the old woman there. She wasn't even blending in with the side of her house. Perplexed, Jemma went around to the back. The stone bench was empty. No sign that anyone was around.

Jemma's heart hammered. *The old woman must be inside.* She figured she had no choice but to knock on the front door. She returned to the front of the house and knocked twice. No answer. She didn't hear movement inside, either. "Well, she couldn't have gone anywhere!" Jemma exclaimed. "Could she?"

Jemma turned, feeling hopeless, and halted in her tracks. Her eyes grew wide. Her heart pounded so hard she could hear it above the wind. Several yards away, walking along the edge of the forest, a man was staggering away from her. Jemma had never seen anyone but Mama B and her father up on this mountain. What was alarming, however, wasn't that she saw a stranger, but that the stranger looked like he was from another time. He was young, perhaps in his thirties, and he wore a US military uniform—and not a modern one. Jemma recognized its era. She had seen the men in the photographs in Harv's diner wearing the same kind of clothing.

"World War II," Jemma murmured. She couldn't believe her eyes. A second later, the man disappeared into the dark trees.

The next instant, Jemma gave a sharp cry when a thin,

wrinkly hand touched her shoulder. "Hush, child," Mama B admonished. Jemma turned to find the old woman standing in the open doorway. "Jumpy like a rabbit today, aren't you, dearie?" She tsked and shook her head.

"Did you see that?" Jemma asked. She pointed a trembling finger at the trees.

Mama B followed her finger and frowned. "I don't see anything but all the damn squirrels, child, though you look like you've seen a ghost." She chuckled and turned toward the interior. "So many squirrels lately, my dear, skittering about my window in the morning and waking me up."

Jemma didn't find that the least bit amusing. *What if I did see a ghost?* she wondered.

Mama B turned as if Jemma had spoken her thought aloud and narrowed her eyes. She seemed to be searching for something in Jemma. The younger woman didn't like how it felt, like she could see right through her.

Mama B went back into the house without a word, beckoning for Jemma to follow. The girl stood on the porch, unsure if she had read the old woman's signal correctly. Mama B turned. "Well, are you coming or not, child? I've made tea and fresh bread, and I don't intend on eating it all by myself."

"You mean I can come inside?" Jemma stammered. She forgot about the man she had seen go into the forest.

Mama B was already down the hall. She called over her shoulder, "It'll be cold if you keep dawdling on my doorstep!"

Jemma stepped inside. She noticed changes within it. Before, everything had been covered in dust. The curtains had been drawn. Now, the curtains were opened to allow the dim light of the autumn day to filter in. Though the house was still unkempt, the cobwebs had been swept away. Overturned items had been righted. What shocked Jemma the most, however, were the empty walls. All those painted portraits with the eyes painted out were gone. Not even the frames were left.

Did I imagine them? she wondered. She could not picture the old woman taking them down by herself. Maybe she'd had help from the ghost by the forest. Jemma shuddered and hurried after Mama B into the kitchen where, sure enough, tea and bread awaited her.

Jemma had never been one for tea or coffee, but when she sipped from the steaming cup Mama B put before her, she felt like she had never tasted anything better. The old woman smiled at her. "I made it for you. When the rain stopped, I knew you would be coming."

It was as if Mama B had forgotten Jemma's breach of trust. The younger woman set the teacup down. "I came to apologize. I should have never intruded into your home."

Mama B nodded and stared into her cup for a long moment. "Well, dearie, I suppose it is my fault too." She looked up and gave Jemma a tired smile. "Why should I expect you to trust me if I try to keep secrets from you?"

Jemma shifted. Mama B's words made her uncomfortable. What secrets was she referring to? The woman gestured at their surroundings. "Truth is, I was embarrassed to have you see my home. Ever since people stopped coming here, I let it fall into disarray. I see now, though, that it will never return to how it was unless I have help." She reached for Jemma's hand. Mama B's touch was firm and warm. Jemma calmed down. The tea helped, too…

somehow. "I need your help, child. We must trust one another again."

Jemma nodded and swallowed a lump that had formed in her throat. She understood where the old woman was coming from, but that didn't make her any less alarmed about the missing portraits and the strange qualities of the house. She decided to set her wariness aside for the time being. She wanted to help the older woman, but more than that, she needed Mama B's help.

Mama B gave Jemma a knowing smile. "You didn't come here to apologize. You came to see about your friend. How is she?"

How does she always know things before I bring them up? Jemma wondered. It was less surprising and more alarming now. She obliged Mama B and told her about Easter's condition. "She's doing better with the paste, but I'm wondering if there's something else that could help her."

Mama B's brows rose. "What might that be?"

Jemma hesitated. She wasn't sure how much she wanted to reveal. *Why can't I tell her? Of all people, she'll be the last to call me crazy,* Jemma thought. She didn't want to say too much of it out loud for fear that doing so would make the reason for Easter's affliction real. The last thing Jemma wanted to believe in was a harmful supernatural creature. She didn't want the rumors of supernatural goings-on to be proven.

"Well," Jemma started, "I'm looking to experiment a little." She shrugged, trying to make her statement nonchalant. "I like chemistry and biology, you know. I'd like to experiment with the kind of herbs you've shown me how to harvest."

Mama B's eyes narrowed. "What kind of herbs, dear?"

Jemma swallowed hard. "I'm interested in dill and jewelweed." She shifted. "Maybe some other things too?" She couldn't remember the whole recipe for the boo hag repellent. "You told me jewelweed could be used for rashes. I'm thinking about making creams for a natural skincare regimen." Then, remembering that Easter had been brought up, Jemma added, "My friend's illness gives her rashes sometimes."

Mama B looked perplexed. She did not answer right away. Instead, she shuffled over to the kitchen window, glanced at the sky, and murmured, "Clouds are heavy today."

The younger woman also looked outside. The sunlight, which had been streaming through the windows a few minutes ago, was blocked by dark clouds. The wind had also picked up; Jemma could see it tearing at the trees. She felt chilly just watching the weather change. The sky looked like it would send rain at any second. Jemma found that odd since the weather reports she had consulted before leaving had told her they wouldn't see rain for another few days.

"Best you return home, child," Mama B told her. "Before the rain comes down too hard." She shuffled out of the room and up the stairs to the second floor. Jemma stood in the kitchen for a long moment, wondering what to do. She heard a door close upstairs.

"Might as well go home," she muttered, annoyed with the old woman for not giving her an answer about the herbs she wanted. As Jemma walked into the hall, she noticed an open door and stairs leading down into darkness. The cellar. That was where Mama B kept her herbs. She glanced at the flight of stairs Mama B had taken to the second floor. She couldn't hear any sounds from upstairs.

It would be easy to slip down there and take what she needed. Conflict simmered within her. She and Mama B had just begun to repair their trust. Was she willing to break it again so soon? She thought about Easter and what she had read in the journals and knew she had to try to help her friend.

Jemma went down into the cellar, which was cold and dark. She found a switch that turned on a dangling light bulb, which flickered. The sound of distant thunder reached her ears. She had to move quickly.

Shelves lined all four walls of the cellar and upon them were glass jars containing herbs. Each was labeled. The handwriting on the labels struck Jemma as familiar. She found the jar labeled Dill and the other labeled jewelweed and hoped she wasn't missing anything. Since she had her backpack, she stuffed both jars inside.

Jemma climbed back up the stairs. It wasn't until she was outside the house that she remembered she had left the light on in the cellar. "Shit! Well, too late now." She glanced at the sky. The weather wasn't going to give her any more time. She had to go home now or be stuck on Mama B's porch until it let up.

The sky was almost black. It was eerier than it had been the first day she came to Gran's Rest. Jemma looked toward the forest. To her relief, the man in the uniform was not around.

She headed down the mountain, her backpack bouncing as she went. The wind picked up, scattering her dark hair across her face. Heavy, pelting rain poured from the sky. "This is what I get," she muttered through clenched teeth. By the time she got home, she would be soaked. She was already cold. "I'm a thief, and this is my punishment."

Still, she forged on. It was for Easter, she thought. She wondered if she *was* doing this for Easter. Or was she doing it for herself? Maybe she was trying to find answers, and she was willing to steal to get them. Those thoughts made her uncomfortable. She shoved them away.

The rest of her journey was tortuous. The ground became slick and muddy. The rain was so heavy that she couldn't see more than a foot or two in front of her. At long last, she came to the paved road. "Not much farther now," she assured herself, but she had a feeling it wouldn't have started raining if she hadn't stolen from Mama B and broken her trust again.

Jemma arrived home, soaking wet and shivering. She pulled her dripping clothes off as fast as she could so she could begin brewing. After she collected the journal pages with the recipe, she set to work. She groaned as she read it. Turned out brewing boo hag repellent would take all night. It required her constant attention and frequent stirring.

In addition, the process proved to be very smelly. On their own, jewelweed and dill smelled fine, but combined, they were horrible.

"An animal might as well have died in here and rotted for days," Jemma muttered. She put a clothespin on her nose and continued to stir. She was so absorbed in making sure she was doing everything right that she did not notice the rain going away until the house was silent except for the sound of the hissing flames of the burner as the pot of brew simmered.

Jemma's eyes were sore after being open for so long. She was so fucking tired, but she couldn't go to sleep until it was done. She needed to complete her task before her father returned home the next day. "I also need to find a way to get this smell out of the house, or I'll have to kill an animal and frame it for the odor." It wasn't a bad idea, but keeping secrets from her father was beginning to get exhausting.

It had never been like this before. What was making her act like this? She couldn't put her finger on a reason, and that bothered her.

At long last, Jemma thought the brew was done. She put the instructions away and opened the window so the smell would be replaced by the scent of plants after the rain. It wafted in, cooling Jemma's sweaty face and neck. Before passing out, she sent Easter a text.

I have something that will help, I think. Come by tomorrow before you go to school.

She wanted her friend to show up before Tad did. Her dad didn't need to know about this yet, not until she was sure it would help Easter. She intended to go up to the loft and get into bed, but she fell asleep at the kitchen table before another thought could form.

A knock on the front door the following morning woke Jemma.

She groaned in pain because of her stiff back and neck and realized she'd fallen asleep at the kitchen table. At least the house smelled a little better. She staggered to the door, still groggy, and opened it to find Easter standing on the porch. She smiled. "Morning, Jemma. I got your message."

Jemma glanced beyond Easter to see Val waiting in his old beater truck. "We've got to get to school, though, so this needs to be quick," the girl added.

"Yes, I'll go grab it," Jemma answered. More awake now, she fetched the jar containing the brew and handed it to Easter.

The other girl stared at it for a long moment. "Is this from Mama B?"

Jemma hesitated. It was, in a way. She nodded. "Keep using the paste I gave you, but use this too. It should help with sleep." It wasn't a lie; it just wasn't the whole truth. It would help if what Jemma had read in the journals was accurate, and Easter's illness was due to a boo hag.

The girl wrapped her arms around Jemma. "Thank you. You're such a good friend. I've never had one quite like you." She pulled back, still smiling.

Jemma squeezed the girl's shoulder. "Don't thank me until you've tried it." She watched as Easter climbed back into the truck and Val drove away. Jemma's heart beat faster than normal. She crossed her fingers, hoping to God or whatever supernatural beings might be watching her that it would work.

CHAPTER TWELVE

Jemma found it difficult to focus on anything else over the next few days. Tad came back but so did the rain, and she couldn't go back to Gran's Rest to work until it passed. She was relieved since she wasn't sure if Mama B had found out yet that she'd stolen from her. She felt queasy when she thought about it. The old woman knew many things Jemma didn't think she was supposed to know. She doubted two missing jars of herbs had escaped her notice.

Mama B wasn't the only one who might be disappointed in Jemma. Tad came into the kitchen one morning looking concerned. "It looks like you're not keeping up with your assignments very well, Jem." He sat down across from her at the table. Jemma had been staring at her chemistry textbook for an hour at this point but hadn't taken a single note. She couldn't even focus on her favorite subject. "Everything all right?" he asked.

Jemma met his eyes and nodded. "Yeah, everything's fine." She paused, not wanting to leave her father completely in the dark. "Well, mostly fine. I'm having a hard time focusing."

Worry must have been clear across her face. "What's bothering you?" Tad asked.

"Easter," Jemma answered truthfully. She was anxious to hear if the new brew had helped, but she hadn't heard a word from Easter or Val, not even a hello or a "Meet us at Harv's at 6?" Easter didn't owe Jemma an update on the medicine, but for her not to say anything was concerning. Jemma hadn't known her very long, but it wasn't like Easter McCarthy to not reach out.

Tad gave his daughter an encouraging smile. "I'm glad you and Easter have become close enough for you to be concerned about her well-being, but sometimes there's nothing we can do."

Except I did do something, Jemma thought. For days, she'd been fighting the urge not to pester Easter about how she was feeling. Maybe her friend didn't want her illness to be a topic of conversation. Jemma had never had an illness like Easter's, but she imagined talking about it all the time would be exhausting.

She was probably being ridiculous. Just because some old journal said boo hags were real didn't mean they were or that Easter was being stalked by one. Still, Jemma couldn't shake the images that came to her mind when she considered the situation. What if the repellent she'd made ran out before Easter got rid of the boo hag?

Jemma forced herself not to think about it anymore. She had to pass her upcoming chemistry test.

"You need to get out of the house and get some fresh air," Tad suggested, drawing Jemma out of her trance. "The rain is supposed to let up tomorrow. Maybe you can go back to work then." He got up and left both the table and the kitchen, leaving her alone with her chemistry book.

Though she dreaded finding out that Mama B knew she'd taken herbs from the cellar, she had to admit she missed being on the mountain.

As Tad had said, the rain had dissipated by the next morning. He drove her to Gran's Rest before going back to the house to work. Mama B was sitting on the porch, prepared to greet father and daughter before Jemma began her work for the day. She was as cheerful and snarky with Tad as ever and didn't give Jemma a look that suggested she didn't trust her anymore.

They began clearing the rest of the early autumn mushrooms without any conversation, which relieved Jemma. Mama B didn't seem inclined to bring up her stealing, even if she did know about it. She gave Jemma a new jar of paste, too. "For your friend. I forgot to give you more when you were here last. I hope your friend has been feeling better."

"Yeah, me too," Jemma murmured. It had been a week since she'd given Easter the concoction she had brewed, and she'd still had no word from her or her brother. Jemma continued to think about it throughout the workday, which distracted her from her tasks. Several times, Mama B had to correct her.

"You're not focusing today, child. That's quite all right. It happens to all of us, but why don't you go home early."

Jemma nodded and called her father. When he asked how her day had been, she forced a smile and mentioned how the weather had cooperated. Tad, however, could see past her façade. "Maybe you can grab dinner with Easter and Val tonight," he suggested.

Jemma would have liked nothing better, but she didn't want to push. "I have to finish chemistry, Dad. Maybe another time."

A couple of hours later, Tad ordered pizza, but Jemma hardly noticed it as she poured herself into her homework. A knock on the door jolted her attention away from her studies. She heard her father open it and give someone a cheerful greeting.

"One second. I'll ask her." Tad appeared in the kitchen. "It looks like the McCarthys want to go to Harv's after all." He wore a broad smile as if their arrival had come about because he'd spoken it into existence. "And since you don't seem to want your pizza, you might as well."

Jemma's head snapped up. All of a sudden, she didn't care about her chemistry test. Finally, Easter had come to see her. But why hadn't she texted or called first? It was strange for Easter to just show up. Despite that, Jemma pulled on her jacket and shoes and met Easter at the door. Val was in the truck, waiting for them.

She stopped short at the sight of her friend. Easter wasn't smiling. Her face was grim, and her arms were folded across her chest. She looked worse than ever. "Hey, Jemma, we need to go to Harv's to talk."

Jemma's brow creased. She didn't like Easter's tone of voice, which was cold and firm. She seemed more energized, less frail, and a little stronger. Her energy, however, was directed at Jemma in an unfriendly manner. There was something about Easter's dark eyes that made her skin crawl. Fighting to hide her nervousness, Jemma nodded. "Let's go. I'll just tell my dad first."

The ride into town was silent. Jemma could feel the tension in the air. She wanted to ask what was wrong, but Val had the radio turned up, and she would have had to shout to be heard. He hadn't so much as looked at Jemma since she got in her car. The McCarthys, it seemed, were not her best friends today.

What the hell was going on? She had gotten up this morning thinking she'd have an unpleasant encounter with Mrs. Brickellwood, not the McCarthys.

Jemma might have been anxious, but Harv's French toast platter was spectacular enough to help her fight the knot forming in her chest. After laboring at Gran's Rest and studying, she had worked up an appetite. She ate like she was famished. Easter and Val made small talk but seemed more friendly toward their waitress. The two ordered plenty of food, and Jemma was surprised to watch Easter eat at the same rate she and Val did. Had the boo hag deterrent worked? Easter was eating like it had.

That didn't make Jemma feel any better. If it had worked, it meant boo hags were real. What did that say about the rest of the supernatural references in the journal? Jemma fought hard not to shudder at the thought.

After their waitress had refilled their sodas, Easter looked Jemma in the eye and began the talk they had come here for. "I felt a difference after the first night I took that sleeping aid you gave me." Easter didn't sound grateful or relieved.

Jemma's fork paused over her French toast. Her

appetite vanished at the look on Easter's face. This wasn't going to be a fun conversation.

Easter folded her hands together on the table. Val kept silent, but he seemed to know what Easter was going to say. "Truth is, I didn't tell anyone, not even Val, until yesterday. I felt like I was approaching the end of my fight with whatever the hell is wrong with me. Before I took what you gave me, I felt like my strength was giving out and the disease was digging out the last bits of me while I was still breathing. After that first night, though, I felt a little better. Not all that much better, mind you," Easter said with a dark chuckle, "but less hollowed-out. I could see a light at the end of the tunnel or some shit."

Jemma hadn't heard Easter talk like this before. *So what went wrong?* she wanted to ask. She didn't have to. Easter continued, "After a few more days, I felt stronger, more like my old self before I found out about my illness." Easter slipped off the black beanie she was wearing to reveal golden stubble on her scalp.

Jemma couldn't believe it. Easter's hair was growing back. She hadn't expected blonde hair. Val's hair was raven-feather black. Both of them had dark, serious eyes.

Here, Val chimed in. "I noticed she was acting different, more like her old self, so I asked her what was going on."

"Val is concerned," Easter interrupted. "He thinks the medicine shouldn't work that fast. He wanted to tell our parents, but I didn't want to give them false hope. That's why we're talking to you. What the hell did you give me?"

Jemma was taken aback. If Easter felt so much better, shouldn't she be grateful instead of paranoid? She stammered but could make no coherent response.

Seeing her expression, Val intervened. "What Easter and I are concerned about is not the medicine you gave her but more the rate at which it is working. Why have you been able to come up with a medicine that works when all her doctors can't?"

Easter eyed Jemma with a hard expression. They were suspicious. Jemma didn't know how to feel about that. She wanted to celebrate the success of the brew, but she didn't want to tell them about the boo hag. All of a sudden, the French toast she had eaten wasn't sitting so well.

"Well," Jemma started, "Mama B asked about your symptoms and mentioned something about haints, but I didn't know what she meant. She gave me herbs, and I—" Easter's weak laugh cut her off. Val shifted, looking uncomfortable. He had chosen to sit on the other side of the booth beside his sister instead of across from her like he usually did.

"Haints are ghosts or spirits," Easter explained when Jemma looked confused. She said it as if it were obvious. "They aren't very friendly."

"Most of the time," Val pointed out, "haints bring down curses or consort with boogers or witches."

Jemma chose to ignore the part about witches. She wasn't going to listen to any more shit about Mama B being one. "What the hell is a booger?"

The word sounded funny to her. Voice shaking, Val told her, "They're creepy things that have proper bodies. Haints don't have bodies of their own; they steal others'. Boogers are as unnatural as they come. There are tons of names for them: mowgs, raw head, bloody bones. So many that I don't think what we call it is the real name." He shrugged. "That's the word I've heard people use the most."

This time, when Jemma shuddered, she didn't try to hide it. "What about boo hags? Have you heard of those?"

Val's eyes widened. Easter's narrowed. The brother answered, "Boo hags are the worst kind of witches, those who have gone too far in their dark magics that they've become more like boogers than humans."

Easter laughed again. The sound made Jemma uncomfortable. She seemed to know something Jemma didn't. "We're talking about this shit like they're real, but they aren't. We know they aren't real because we aren't crazy."

The McCarthy siblings stared at Jemma for a long moment. She tried to think of a response, but she didn't know how much to tell them. She didn't want to explain that a boo hag was afflicting her with an illness modern medicine couldn't cure. When she didn't answer, Val muttered to Easter, "Told you so." His face had paled to the color of milk.

Jemma opened her mouth to object or explain; she didn't know which. Before she could say another word, Val interrupted.

"There's more, and I'm going to sound batshit-crazy for saying this, but I know what I saw." He swallowed hard and looked like he was going to throw up the dinner he had eaten. "One night years ago, when Easter was starting to get sick, I heard her whimpering in her room. It sounded like she was having a bad dream. I went to her door and looked in." He gulped, looking sicker still. "I saw a dark shape, like a bent-over dark woman, straddling Easter's chest."

Finally, Easter couldn't keep her head up. She stared at her lap.

Jemma's heart hammered. She felt sick as Val told his story too.

Val continued, "I tried to cry out, but my voice stuck in my throat. I made a sound, but it wasn't loud enough. It drew the thing's attention, and the next thing I knew, her bedroom door slammed in my face hard enough for the wind from it to knock me over. The house felt like it was rattling. My parents thought we had an earthquake or something."

He shook his head. "I knew that wasn't it. I was scared, but everyone thought I was babbling about some shadow I thought was a woman. They told me I was dreaming and blamed the goose egg on my head on running into a closed door while sleepwalking. I know I saw something, though. I just know it." His conviction was clear in his voice. Jemma believed him, though the whole thing sounded insane.

Easter's gaze slid up, but she didn't look Val or Jemma in the eye. "I didn't want to believe him, but now..." She couldn't finish her sentence.

After Val's horror story, Jemma knew she had no choice but to share what she had found. The story spilled from her lips, starting with the journal and ending with the confession about stealing from Mama B. The McCarthys listened raptly. Jemma hoped no one else could hear their conversation. They would know the three of them were odder than they were already perceived to be.

"I just wanted to help," Jemma finished. "I saw it as a

Hail Mary thing. I didn't think it would work, but now that we know it does..." She struggled to finish the sentence.

Pale and wide-eyed, Val did it for her. "There are a lot more questions and concerns now."

Jemma's mind was in turmoil, but Easter's face had changed. She looked stricken with worry. Val still looked pale but seemed happy that he had been right. All those years ago, he *had* seen something. It hadn't been "just a dream."

Jemma glanced at her watch and saw that it wasn't much past 7:00, although it was very dark outside. Darkness came sooner to the small mountain town than it did to cities beyond the peaks. Jemma had the feeling that the darkness here was an entity of its own, arriving when it wanted, to be driven away only by the force of the sun. She remembered walking down from Gran's Rest alone that first night and wishing the darkness didn't feel so close. She had decided she'd never go to or from the place in the dark again. That decision, however, was about to be changed.

Tad won't be calling until after ten. I have time to fix this. Jemma swallowed hard and forced her words out despite her misgivings. "We should go to Gran's Rest right now and talk to Mama B."

CHAPTER THIRTEEN

Neither of the McCarthys was enthused about Jemma's suggestion to go up the mountain after dark to talk to an old woman who lived alone and was deemed a dangerous witch by many of the locals.

Jemma presented the argument that those who were afraid of Mrs. Eloise Brickellwood didn't know her, and she did. Still, she was also wary of the drive up the mountain in the dark. She tried to shake it off, but after hearing Val's story about the boo hag, she felt like a little girl waiting for monsters to come out from under her bed.

To Jemma's surprise, Easter was the most nervous about the plan. Val jumped in to help Jemma convince her to go with them. "She's the only one who won't think we're crazy. We have to try." Val gave Jemma a pleading look. "At least, I hope that's the case."

Jemma tried to appear confident and cleared her throat. "Either Mama B is a misunderstood old lady, or we're going to visit someone who might know what this supernatural mystery is about. It can't hurt, either way."

Finally, Easter relented, but she appeared anxious during the drive up the mountain. Val clutched the steering wheel. The higher they went on the winding road, the more static overpowered the music on the radio. Eventually, Val had to switch the radio off, which left the three of them sitting with only the howling wind outside to sing to them. They had the heat on in the truck, but Jemma still felt cold.

The beater truck was growling when they reached the top of the hill. Val pulled to a stop, and Jemma opened the back door. Instantly, she knew something was wrong. She sensed it before she saw them. Through the trees, blue and red lights flashed. The dirt road showed signs of multiple vehicles having gone up the slope ahead of them.

"What the hell is going on?" Val muttered as he stepped out of the driver's side of the truck.

"I don't know," Jemma answered, her voice shaking.

Easter tried to say something, but what came was a whimper.

Val started forward. Easter's voice croaked to call him back. Curiosity overcame Jemma, though, and she gripped Easter's hand. "Together," she whispered. Once they were through the trees and had stopped in front of the old, faded sign for Gran's Rest, they saw a sheriff's truck, two patrol cars, and the local ambulance, which wasn't an actual ambulance but a modified full-sized van with lights on top.

"No!" Jemma rasped. Her cry didn't carry very far. She started forward. What happened to Mama B? Was she hurt? She looked at the ambulance van, which was open. She didn't see anyone inside it, so she scanned the scene. When her eyes landed on the porch, she was relieved to see the venerable old woman talking to the sheriff while swatting away a pair of paramedics.

They're checking her for injuries! Jemma realized. Fear and relief battled for dominance within her. Mama B looked unharmed for the most part. She made to rush toward the old woman, but one of the deputies stepped in front of her. "Stop right there, young lady." He looked over her shoulder at Val and Easter, who were huddled together. Jemma didn't know if they were more afraid of the police or the old woman. The deputy narrowed his eyes. "You're the McCarthys." He looked Jemma over. "And you and your father are new around here. What brings the three of you up the mountain at this time of night?"

"We're here to see Mrs. Brickellwood. We're friends," Jemma stammered.

The policeman's brows rose. "Friends?" He either doubted the old woman had any friends or that she was friends with teenagers. Jemma didn't want to explain the supernatural aspects of their journey.

"Jemma!" a voice shrieked. She whirled to see Easter pointing ahead. Beside one of the police cars, a deputy stood in the flashing lights. He wasn't alone. In handcuffs, a nasty bruise marring the left side of his face, and his right eye swollen shut, was AJ Kilmer. The deputy shoved him into the backseat.

"What the fucking hell!" Val and Jemma exclaimed in unison. Jemma couldn't believe it. AJ could be a troublemaker, but he'd come up the mountain to cause harm to a little old lady? That was more than crossing the line. She clenched her fists. She wanted nothing more than to punch him like she had the first night she'd laid eyes on him.

"She knows us, sir," Jemma argued desperately. "Well, she knows me, anyway. I work for her!" No amount of pleading changed the deputy's mind, however.

Mama B's voice rose above the teenager's and the policeman's as she called to them. "Robert Arthur Owens, whose birth I shepherded and whose momma's birth I shepherded too, don't you be deciding who can and can't be on my property!"

The deputy responded to the name.

Mama B wasn't finished. "Let those young 'uns up here. They're here to look after an old lady in her distress."

Robert Arthur Owens frowned at the teenagers. "How did you know she was in trouble?"

He had not spoken loud enough for Mama B to hear, but she reacted like she knew what he'd said. "I called 'em! Let 'em come up."

Jemma had never heard the old lady lie, but she was glad she had.

Deputy Owens sighed, moved aside looking like a scolded schoolboy, and motioned for Jemma, Val, and Easter to go up the remaining part of the slope. It did not escape Jemma's notice that Mama B had mentioned bringing the deputy into the world and his mother before him. Once again, she was struck by the strange time thing. The deputy was at least fifty, which meant his mother was around seventy years old, which meant Mrs. Eloise Brickellwood...

Jemma stopped on the first porch step. *She's old as hell.*

Val and Easter halted behind Jemma. They all overheard what the sheriff said to the old lady. "If you're not going to press charges, we'll get a drug test on AJ and get him for possession." The aging sheriff shook his head in disappointment. "The boy is clearly on something, yammering on about his mother. I tell you what. I work hard to keep this county clean of meth and heroin and pills. Not much I can do about reefer, what with all the legalizing and medicalizing and all that bullshit.

"Pardon my language, ma'am, but I'll be damned if somebody's goin' to come into Kalhoun County and start sellin' that poison to our kids." The sheriff looked sad. "I hate to tell the boy's father about this. RJ is a good man. It's a damn shame." He shook his head again. "A damn shame."

Mama B seemed equally dejected. "Do what you must. I'll respect you for it, but the young man is in custody, and I am fine." She glared at the hovering paramedics. "All I ask is that your emergency personnel go on their way and give me a chance to put my guests at ease." She gestured at Jemma, Val, and Easter.

Jemma glanced over her shoulder at the patrol car with AJ in the backseat. She could only see one side of his face, the side with the uninjured eye. She thought about making both sides look the same. It took every ounce of restraint not to stomp over there and give AJ a piece of her mind. Who the hell was he to start shit with an old lady? It was one thing to threaten a teenage girl half his size; it was another to ambush an old woman who lived alone.

Jemma turned back to Mama B as the old woman went on, "Besides, the boy's daddy is headin' to meet you at the county jail since young Deputy Dover gave RJ a call. I know that because I was payin' attention while you were concerned with my wounds, which I don't have."

When Jemma looked the old woman over, Mrs. Brickellwood appeared untouched. "You do remember that the Dovers are kin to the Kilmers, Sheriff?"

The sheriff's face reddened. "Somehow slipped my mind," he muttered. "Thank ya, Mama B, for the reminder. I suppose we'll get out of your hair now. You have a good night."

Mama B gave a final warning glare to the paramedics. "Too late for that. Go on now. You heard the man."

Everyone cleared out. Jemma waited in silence for them to depart. The lights flashed down the slope and out of sight. Jemma watched them until they were gone, then turned to Mama B. She wondered if the old woman had only pretended to be uninjured. Jemma scanned her body, looking for any sign of harm.

Mama B sighed. "I'm guessing you three are wondering what happened."

Jemma was surprised she didn't demand to be told why they were there, but perhaps she already knew. Mama B beckoned them inside. A fire crackled in the hearth. The inside looked cozy, not eerie. Val and Easter looked around with wide eyes. Jemma was relieved her friends wouldn't see all the portraits.

Mama B motioned for them to sit together on a sofa opposite her overstuffed rocking chair. "I was finishing up my pressing and preserving for the day when I heard someone trying to break in through the back door. I thought about getting my old revolver, but then I caught a glimpse of that Kilmer boy through the window, and I decided just to give him a good whack instead." She gestured at a stout walking stick beside the fireplace.

Val and Easter were too distracted by the situation to

react, but Jemma had to stifle her laughter. It was difficult for her to imagine Mama B giving AJ Kilmer a spanking. "Well, his face told me you pulled it off," she heard herself say.

Mama B chuckled. "That wasn't so bad, dearie. I could have done a lot worse." Jemma laughed aloud. She couldn't help it. This was the third time in a few days that AJ Kilmer had been laid low and now by an old woman.

Mama B's amusement faded. "I'm worried for that boy. He's been troublesome for a long time but more so of late."

How does she know that? Jemma wondered. As far as she knew, Mama B never went into town. How did she even know the young man?

Mama B produced a tired smile. "He's been a bad seed since he was a babe, but there's always hope that with enough light and love, even a bad seed can struggle free of its darker predispositions." She shook her head. "Whatever possessed AJ, be it drugs or somethin' else, it doesn't bode well for him." This last remark was murmured more to herself than to the three teenagers sitting across from her. The old woman stared into the fire for a long moment.

Val and Easter still seemed not to know what to think, much less what to do or say. Jemma just waited for Mama B. At last, the old woman looked at her guests. "Well now, I'll fetch us some tea, and then why don't the three of you tell me why you're here?"

CHAPTER FOURTEEN

Jemma didn't know how to start. She swallowed hard when she remembered that telling this story would involve explaining to Mama B that she had stolen from her, breaking her trust once again. Jemma felt sick, but there was no way out of it.

To her surprise, she didn't have to explain. Easter spoke for the first time since arriving at the top of the hill. Her voice was strong, which Jemma had not expected. Her hands were balled into tight fists in her lap. Val still looked like he'd seen a ghost. "I've been sick for a long time, Mama B, and I didn't start to feel better until Jemma brought me something to help." She tried to smile, but it came out as a grimace. "Thank you for giving Jemma the paste and the brew."

Mama B's brows furrowed in confusion at the mention of a brew, and her eyes slid to Jemma. The younger woman couldn't bear to meet her gaze and did not say a word. Not yet, anyway.

Voice faltering, Easter continued, "We've figured my illness isn't normal." She gulped.

Val joined in, his voice shaking as he related to Mama B what he had told Jemma in the diner. The whole time he spoke, Mama B listened intently. Her expression was unreadable, every limb still. Jemma squirmed. She wanted this conversation to end. "We think it might have been a boo hag," Val finished at last.

Mama B looked at Jemma long enough to make the young woman meet her gaze. "Where did you learn about boo hags, child?"

"In-in a journal I f-found in my house," Jemma stammered. "It was with the photo album I showed to you."

"Ah, yes," Mama B replied. She nodded as if she had known that. "And you took what you needed from my cellar to follow the instructions in the journal, yes?"

Slowly, red-faced and ashamed, Jemma nodded.

Mama B's expression changed from unreadable to disappointed to angry. Jemma felt like fleeing, not from fear but because of the heavy press of guilt. At first, Jemma thought the old woman was angry with her for stealing, but she realized that there was far more to Mama B's wrath.

"I'll pay you back. Cash or labor or whatever you need. And I'm sorry—" Jemma began, but the old woman interrupted her.

Mama B shook her head, so disappointed Jemma could not continue. She had never seen anyone so upset, and she could not understand why. "You engaged in the Art, child, and you had no damn idea what you were doing! You engaged in the Art without supervision. That was bad enough, but what is worse is that you used that untested creation to defy something as potent and dangerous as a boo hag! Do you know what you've done?"

Jemma had no clue what the old woman meant, but she knew it wasn't good. In fact, whatever it was, it was very bad.

"The damned creature will know it was used now! She'll come after you, child, if she hasn't already!" Mama B exclaimed.

The air went out of the room. Easter and Val were motionless as their friend was being yelled at. Jemma's eyes welled with tears. What the hell had she done? Not only had she dabbled in the Art, whatever the hell it was, but she had also caused the thing that had been pestering Easter to come and afflict her! On top of all of that, she had made someone she respected very upset with her.

At least her father didn't know. Jemma dreaded the thought of Tad Nox finding out about all this.

Another thought came to her. What if AJ had come up here and broken in to get back at her? She might have put Mrs. Brickellwood in danger because she'd punched the guy the first time she met him.

Mama B's stern look and sterner words forced Jemma's thoughts back to her. "I wish you had come to me." Her tone conveyed her disappointment. "I could have guided you, but now it is trial by fire." She shook her head. "The boo hag is already moving against you."

"How is that so?" Val had found his voice and was desperate for answers.

Mama B answered Val's question but continued to look at Jemma. "I suspect AJ Kilmer's break-in was the first thing that damned creature did. That boy wasn't under the influence of drugs and alcohol. I could tell when I saw him." She shuddered. "The way he shrieked, it didn't sound like a teenage boy. I shoulda known. I shoulda known." Now she spoke as if she were disappointed in herself.

"How did the boo hag know AJ didn't like me, though?" Jemma asked.

Mama B looked at her sharply. "Maybe it had nothing to do with AJ except his current state of mind made him vulnerable to the creature's will. No doubt since you used herbs from my property, the creature sniffed her way up here." She waved her hand at their surroundings. "I've got magic woven all around my home to protect it from something like a boo hag, but that doesn't mean it would keep out a person possessed by her. That boy she got into was hexed good and proper, but them damn police wouldn't have believed me."

"How did the boo hag know it was Jemma, though?" Easter asked the question. Her voice trembled, and her face was full of guilt as if she were taking responsibility for the whole situation. Tears came to her eyes. "It's not Jemma's fault. Not really. I was sick because of the creature, and she was trying to help."

Mama B's face softened. "I know you meant well, Jemma Nox, but having good intentions doesn't mean the results of our choices are good. The boo hag knew it was Jemma because right before the three of you came up the hill, that young man AJ whipped his head in her direction. He snarled like some damn wolf and thrashed, trying to get free."

"Damn," Val muttered.

Jemma couldn't find words. Easter, too, fell silent and looked at the floor where the fire caused the shadows to dance. Mama B was still except for the tapping of a fingernail on her thin chin. Questions swarmed Jemma's mind until she couldn't contain them any longer. One slipped out as she considered their conversation so far. "Do you know anything about the journal I found with the photo album?"

Mama B hesitated. A weighty memory hung behind her eyes in the labyrinth of her mind. Jemma watched her struggle before she nodded. "Yes, child, I know the woman who wrote that journal. It was the woman the photo album belonged to before she died." She sounded sad, but she forged ahead. "She was my sister, a fellow holler witch and a dear woman. I loved her very much."

Jemma couldn't breathe. She exchanged looks with Easter and Val. "S-so, what they s-say is true?" Val stammered. "You *are* a witch."

Mama B gave them a sad smile. "I never denied it."

"A witch," Jemma echoed. It made sense. Only someone with a supernatural element in their existence could be as old as Mama B and still be alive. It explained her knowledge of little-known things when no evidence was produced. And she was not the only witch.

Mama B sniffled. "I've been a witch for as long as anyone who talks about me has known me, and most of what they say is true. Now, I don't want to be talkin' about my sisters, if you don't mind. We have greater concerns at the moment."

Yes, the boo hag. How the hell was she supposed to deal with it?

"Jemma, it's time you become a holler witch yourself so you can fend off the boo hag. There isn't any other way, I'm afraid." She smiled as if she had been waiting for this moment since she'd first laid eyes on the girl.

"A holler witch?" Jemma was incredulous. "How's that different from a regular witch?" She had a hard time picturing herself in a pointy hat, riding a broomstick and stirring things in a cauldron, though she supposed brewing boo hag repellent all night over a stove wasn't very different.

Mama B chuckled. "Yes, a holler witch. A woman who is wood-wise and earth-crafty. I don't say that because of the considerable potential you've shown. Not just anyone can craft an effective boo hag repellant with scanty knowledge from a rambling old book and my careless mutterings."

She glanced from Jemma to the McCarthy siblings, who looked scared out of their minds. "You've shown potential by caring for yourself and your friends. The best witches care for the well-being of others. Remember that, child."

A lump formed in Jemma's throat. How could this be happening? Just today, she had been prepared to defend Mama B against anyone who called her a witch or any other name. Now she sat on top of a hill in an old house and had been told she'd have to become a witch herself to right her mistakes.

If only I had never stolen from her, she thought. *If only I had acted like myself.*

Jemma snapped out of what felt like a daze. *Why the hell do I believe all this?* Until this point, she had been a believer in science, not magic. Mama B might have admitted to being a witch, but what if her kindness was a façade? If what people like AJ Kilmer had said about her was right?

Then her eyes strayed to Easter, and her mind changed. *I caused all this to happen because I tried to help, but I tried alone.* Jemma had to acknowledge that her choices had led her here and she couldn't get out of it by pretending this supernatural talk was mumbo-jumbo.

She felt a weight and gravity upon her that she had only felt at one other point in her life: when her mother decided that being with other people mattered more than being with her daughter. It had been a turning point. Jemma had had to step up and take control of her own life.

This was another turning point, except this time, her father wasn't the only one she needed to protect. She gazed at Easter and Val. She had to help her friends. She didn't want Easter to be sick anymore, and she didn't want to become sick either.

Jemma looked at Mama B. "Tell me what to do."

Since it was late and Jemma's father would be texting and calling soon, Mama B decided that for now, they needed a way to keep the boo hag clear of Jemma, her father, and the McCarthys until they had found a workable solution.

The fire was dying when Mama B rose from her chair and shuffled into the kitchen. Jemma let out a deep breath and looked down to see Easter's warm hand in her own. Whether she held it because she wanted comfort or was trying to give it, Jemma did not know. She was grateful for it either way and happy Easter McCarthy didn't hate her.

The commotion from the kitchen went on for several minutes until Mama B reappeared at last, having cobbled together small pouches that she presented to each of the youths on her sofa. "Inside, you'll find an herbal mixture that'll make the boo hag want to get as far away from your homes as it can." Next, Mama B scribbled a small spiral symbol on two pieces of paper. She handed one to Jemma and the other to Val. "Bury the pouches within a few paces of your front doors, then carve this symbol on the doorframe." She looked at Val. "You have to do it, son, since your sister is too weak and susceptible to the boo hag."

Jemma stared at the pouch for a long moment before asking, "Why won't the boo hag repellent be enough? Couldn't we just make enough for all three of us to use?"

To her surprise, Mama B smiled instead of getting annoyed. "A good witch begins her practice with good questions. You've started on the right foot."

Jemma wasn't sure having a boo hag hunting her was a good footing, but she listened to the wiser, more experienced woman before her.

"The dill and jewelweed," Mama B explained, confirming that she knew exactly what Jemma had taken from her cellar, "will make it so the boo hag is too sick to feed, but it won't keep the angry and determined creature from causing all manner of trouble. Remember what happened tonight, child."

How could I forget? Jemma thought as AJ Kilmer's bruised and swollen face came into her mind.

Mama B continued, "Anyone with a weak mind can be invaded by a boo hag. She'll wear down a strong mind over time." She shook her head sadly. "I've seen very stable-minded people fall to her whims."

Jemma shuddered at the thought. She recalled what she had read in the journal. It seemed like Mrs. Eloise Brickellwood and her sister, who had written the journal, had much experience with boo hags. Now that Mama B had the three teenagers armed, she sent them on their way. "Be here first thing in the morning," she instructed Jemma, "so we can start arming up for the coming fight."

Jemma found it hard to form words. "I don't want to fight. Isn't there another way?"

Mama B scowled. "Fight's coming for you either way, dearie. You can take the hits or hit back, but there's no hiding from it." Her scowl faded, and her features and voice softened. "Besides, I don't figure you're the hiding sort." The Mrs. Brickellwood Jemma stood before now seemed less frail and less sweet. She was stronger, wiser, and more formidable than she had been. She liked this version of Mama B, even if she was a witch and despite the circumstances that brought out this side of her.

Jemma lifted her chin. "I'm not."

Mama B's eyes twinkled. "You will show me that is true beginning tomorrow."

Jemma, Val, and Easter rushed to the truck through the cold October air and remained silent the whole way from Gran's Rest to Jemma's house. It wasn't a tense quiet; it was that none of them knew what to say. Hell, Jemma didn't know what to think or feel, much less how to form words to describe it.

Val pulled into Jemma's driveway. As she climbed out, she turned back to look at her friends. Easter gave her a tired but reassuring smile as if to say, "Stay safe. We're in this together." She watched until the truck was out of sight before she turned, took the deepest breath she'd ever taken, and did as Mama B had instructed.

Jemma worked as fast as she could without messing up the process. She dug a small hole five paces from the front door and re-covered it so it didn't look like anything was buried there. She then etched the symbol on the doorframe where it wouldn't be obvious to her father. After she went in, she shut the door quickly.

"That was a hell of a night!" she muttered. Her words trailed off as she saw her father in the living room. He was asleep in his recliner with the TV on and an open book in his lap. *I'll tell him about the break-in tomorrow but leave out the supernatural shit,* Jemma decided. Her father wouldn't believe it. Jemma wasn't sure she believed it either.

She got ready for bed by undressing, brushing her teeth, and washing her face. As she did, she was tense and ready to bolt. Before going to bed, Jemma added another layer of protection by putting her father's old baseball bat by her bed and a kitchen knife under her pillow. She doubted either one would help her against a boo hag, though. They did nothing but make her feel more paranoid.

As soon as her head hit the pillow, her phone dinged to indicate she had a text. It was from Easter.

We made it home all right, and Val did what Mama B told us. Sleep well, J.

A minute or two passed, then:

And thank you, J. For everything. I know it isn't going according to plan, but when does life ever do that? Haha. No one else would do this for me except Val, of course.

Though she was paranoid, stressed, and terrified about what tomorrow and the following days would bring, Jemma was warmed by her friend's message. She tried to go to sleep. It wasn't easy, but gradually, she drifted into an uneasy sleep with strange images and feelings in her dreams. They were like what Easter had described as part of her afflictions the whole time she had been ill.

It hadn't even been a week since Jemma had made the choice to brew the boo hag repellant, and already she was paying for it.

CHAPTER FIFTEEN

Jemma awoke with a start in her darkened room. A loud noise had awakened her but faded before she was fully conscious. Her brain tried to sort out how she could remember a sound she hadn't been awake for.

She wondered what she had been dreaming about but couldn't remember. Jemma hadn't so much been awakened by the sound as felt it in the center of her being. Maybe that was where her heart was, but it was deeper.

There was something in her room, she decided. Something that wasn't supposed to be.

She climbed out of bed and scooped up her father's baseball bat. Whatever had tried to get in had failed, but despite that, every sense was dialed up to eleven as she attempted to sort out what she was feeling. Jemma paused at the top of the ladder and peered down. She couldn't hear anything but her father's snoring from his recliner, where he was still asleep.

I should go back to bed, she told herself. *I'm imagining things because I've had a hell of a night*. She tried to convince herself she was being paranoid, but she couldn't shake her fear. She tried to get back into bed, but her body wouldn't let her. "Fine," she hissed under her breath, "I'll go take a look." Jemma picked up the bat once more, slid down the ladder, and stalked to the front of the house through the hallway, past her father in the living room.

With her apprehension rising, Jemma peered through the front window at the porch and the lawn. The yard was dark except for the dim glow of the porch light, which only illuminated the grass a few feet beyond the steps. Trees grew in clumps on the left side of the house. She looked toward the road and gasped. She spied a shadowy figure righting itself on the front lawn and darting across her yard as if it had changed its mind about where it was going. The figure was too distorted for her to tell what it was. What the hell had she seen?

The yard returned to its normal state: empty and with nothing unusual stirring in it. Although Jemma couldn't tell what the figure was, she was certain it had been the boo hag. The very air trembled around her. Whatever wards had sprung up as a result of Jemma burying the pouch of herbs and carving the spiral symbol in the door had worked to keep the creature out.

Jemma stood motionless, experiencing both terror and relief. A monster had almost come into her house, but it had run away. She straightened and evened her breathing. *I'm not crazy for believing Mama B. She was right. The boo hag is* real.

Jemma looked out the window for a long time, but she

did not see the shadowy figure again. Thanks to the thoughts raging in Jemma's mind, she failed to notice that her father's snoring had ceased. She didn't hear his footsteps or him clearing his throat. A hand landed on her shoulder, and a startled shriek escaped her mouth. She whirled, baseball bat held tight in her hand. She was ready to swing.

"Whoa, Jem!" Tad called.

Once she realized it was her father, Jemma lowered the bat and breathed a sigh of relief. "Dad, I'm sorry."

Tad stepped closer, worry creasing his brow. He looked at the bat in her hand. Recognition crossed his face when he realized the bat was his. "Jemma, what's wrong?" There was worry in his voice.

Jemma scrambled for an answer. She glanced at the front door, knowing how ridiculous she looked standing there with her father's bat in her hands. "I heard something and I thought someone was breaking in, but it turned out to be nothing." She forced a tired smile. "Sorry for waking you."

"Yeah," Tad replied with a nervous chuckle. "You were muttering things under your breath."

"I was?" Jemma didn't remember that part.

Tad chuckled again. "You're not sleepwalking, are you? You haven't done that since you were twelve."

"What was I muttering?"

Tad gently took the bat from Jemma's hands. "Something about how you're not crazy, and she was right." He cocked his head. "Who were you talking about?"

Jemma didn't answer, but Tad didn't seem very

concerned about what she had been muttering. Still a little groggy, he gave his daughter a concerned squint before placing his hand on her shoulder again. "Next time, Jem, wake me up before you head off to face danger." He winked. "Plus, I've swung this bat before. You haven't."

They had better weapons in the house than the old baseball bat, but she didn't know if a gun or a knife would work on a boo hag. She had another question for Mama B: how the hell did she kill a boo hag?

"Sorry, Dad. I didn't think." She considered telling him about AJ's attempt to break-in at Gran's Rest, but before she could, Tad tugged her down the hall by the arm. "Back to bed, Jem. Can't believe I fell asleep in that chair for so long. My neck is stiff."

Jemma paused at the base of the ladder. She felt like she needed to tell her father *something*. What, she did not know, but it felt strange to leave him in the dark. Her life had taken a significant turn, but she felt like she couldn't talk about it.

"Dad…" she began.

"In the morning, Jem. We're both dead-tired."

Jemma couldn't agree more. She smiled wearily. "Goodnight, Tad."

"Goodnight, Jem."

Jemma found it even more difficult to fall asleep this time than she had earlier. Her sleep was uneasy. She felt like she had just fallen asleep when the morning light filtered through the loft window and illuminated her pillow.

She still didn't believe everything that had happened the day before. She felt like she was waking up from a nightmare. Jemma didn't decide to get up; she just did. Before she knew it, she had opened her closet door and pulled out the box containing the loose journal pages. She scanned the cramped writing. This was real. Every bit of it was real. As she rifled through the pages, her fingers paused over something different. Instead of a sheet of paper with blurred writing, she peered at a faded photograph.

Jemma gasped as she pulled it out. It showed three women in their thirties. The one standing in the middle was very familiar. Those eyes could not be mistaken as belonging to anyone but Mrs. Eloise Brickellwood. The women on either side of her seemed just as strong but in different ways. The woman on the left looked feminine and wise. The woman on the right looked boyish with a short haircut and angular features. She wore trousers, whereas the woman on the left wore a dress trimmed in lace. The woman in the center, Mama B, looked like a combination of the two. She wore trousers and a blouse. Her long curly hair was pulled back from her face, and her eyes were dark and fierce. The corners of her lips were quirked as if someone had told a joke before the photo was taken.

Jemma recalled what Mama B had told her, Val, and Easter the night before. She had had a sister, another holler witch. Had she had two sisters? One of these women, Jemma supposed, could be Ms. Mabel Doire, who used to own this home. She wondered which one was Ms. Doire and if she had written the journals.

"I need to do more research," Jemma muttered. She opened her laptop next and typed in "holler witch." Next, she found a pen and paper and scribbled down facts she found online. Her first hit was a site labeled Granny Witches of Appalachia. When she selected the article, she read about how "back in the old days," hospitals were too far away for those who lived in the mountains, so they went to women who could heal with their knowledge of herbalism. Were holler witches specific to this area? "And why would women who make medicine from plants and herbs be called witches?" Jemma wondered aloud.

Shuffling from the floor below redirected Jemma's attention. Her father was awake and would be ready to drive her up the mountain to Gran's Rest any minute. Jemma closed her laptop and shoved the journal pages, along with the photograph, back into the closet.

In the kitchen, Tad offered Jemma a plate of eggs.

"Dad, I have to tell you what happened last night." She dove into the story, talking about how, after dinner with Val and Easter, they had gone up to Gran's Rest so her friends could meet her employer. When they got there, however, they found that the place had been broken into and that AJ Kilmer was the culprit. She left out the part where Mama B beat the kid black and blue with nothing but a staff. Jemma wondered if there had been a magical element to the ordeal, even if it was just increased strength for the old woman.

"I knew that boy was bad news," Tad growled as his hand clenched around his coffee mug. There wasn't coffee in it, only orange juice, but he liked to drink from a mug in the morning while he read the paper. "Funny, there's nothing in the paper about it."

Jemma shrugged. "I don't think Mama B wanted attention brought to it."

"Still," Tad responded. "That boy ought to be locked up if he's gonna try to harm teenage girls and old women."

"The police got him." Jemma rose. "I need to go help her clean up and fix a few things AJ broke." That wasn't the truth, but Jemma couldn't bring herself to tell her father she was going to the mountain for witch training. It wasn't the kind of future he had imagined for her when they'd decided to move here.

Tad smiled. "I can take some time off and come help if you want." He wiggled his eyebrows. "I'm pretty handy, you know."

Tad Nox was the last person Jemma wanted to witness her training, regardless of what it entailed. *I'm not ready to explain all that shit yet,* she thought. Aloud, she told her father, "It's a sweet offer, Tad, but I think it would be better if it was just me."

Tad nodded. "I understand." He looked up from his plate and gave his daughter a kind but concerned look. "Look, Jem, I understand why you were up in the middle of the night. I'm proud of you for how brave and kind you are."

Jemma swallowed hard. Her father assumed she had been armed with the baseball bat because she feared AJ Kilmer was breaking in even though he had been led away in the back of a police car. She didn't feel quite so brave or kind, knowing she was lying to her father, but she was relieved to discover he was taking it well. "Thanks, Tad. I'm ready to go whenever you are."

Tad smiled. "Up the mountain we go!"

Jemma got distracted during the drive. Her father's favorite thing to do while driving the winding mountain roads was to sing, *"She'll be comin' round the mountain when she comes!"* at the top of his lungs. He did it with such enthusiastic cheer that Jemma couldn't resist laughing. "Sing with me, Jem! *She'll be comin' round the mountain when she comes!"*

Gran's Rest came into sight a moment later, and Jemma was spared from having to sing the second verse. Tad's song faded as Jemma got out of the truck. She waved at him as he turned and went back down the mountain.

The autumn air was crisp and warm today. The sun beamed down upon them. Jemma was glad for it. The weather lifted her spirits even though the daunting task of training lay before her. Mama B stood on the porch, looking stronger and sterner than she had last night. She was no longer the frail old woman who had sat on the porch swing waiting for help. Mama B was dressed as if she were ready for a hike. Her stout walking stick was in her hand. In the other, she held a leather pack. As Jemma approached, she tossed her the leather pack. "We'll be spending some time in the woods today, dearie, and you'll need everything that's in there."

Jemma replaced her backpack with the leather pack. "How long will we be gone?"

"As long as it takes." Mama B's voice was firm. "This kind of training won't be done in one day or even two, child. It's going to take a few weeks." Jemma's heart dropped into her stomach. That meant weeks of waking in the middle of the night with the sensation that something was trying to get to her. She didn't want to go through that again, but it would be better than what Val had described when he'd seen the boo hag sucking the life out of his sister.

Mama B produced another walking stick, seemingly from thin air, and handed it to her apprentice. Jemma Nox wasn't just a groundskeeper anymore. She took the staff. It seemed ancient and looked like it had been made for more than walking. It had carvings similar to the one Jemma had etched into her doorframe the night before. *Will this staff help keep me safe?* she wondered.

Mama B started toward the woods. Apprehension welled within Jemma. She had the feeling she was about to step into something that was way above her head. Mama B called over her shoulder as she marched toward the trees, "The first thing to remember is that what makes a holler witch powerful is her connection to the living world."

She turned and winked at her young apprentice. "I'm willing to bet that, by the end of today, you'll be cussing that connection with every fiber of your being."

Jemma didn't find the woman's words amusing, but Mama B seemed to think the young woman's training was what she deserved. *I do deserve this*, Jemma thought. *I tried to fix something on my own, and it didn't work.* She thought about her parents and how she had tried to fix them. It had been a heavy task for someone so young. That hadn't worked out either. Feeling defeated, Jemma picked up her pace and followed Mama B into the forest.

The trees were old and bowed over her in an arch. Jemma pulled her jacket tighter around her. Under the trees, the sun was less able to warm her. A chilly wind came through, ruffling her hair. Without realizing it, Jemma pressed closer to Mama B.

The old woman glanced over her shoulder once more. "And one more thing: no more of that sugary plastic garbage you keep sticking in your mouth."

Cursing, Jemma emptied her pockets of hard candies.

Looked like more was going to change.

CHAPTER SIXTEEN

Dear Diary, Jemma wrote. She groaned and scratched it out. "I'm not in middle school, writing about a boy I have a crush on," she muttered.

After her first day of training with Mama B, she had decided to keep a journal like the one in her closet that had started this whole thing. It helped her thoughts be less muddled and gave her a place to talk about her lessons without having to confide in her father.

> *Mama B wasn't lying when she told me I'd be cursing the living world and my connection to it after only a day of training. Every part of it is fucking terrible, but she is right about one thing: I do have a connection. I've had it since the beginning of my time with her, maybe even before.*

Jemma couldn't explain it. She felt an ease in learning about the wildlife around Gran's Rest that she had never possessed with anything else. Understanding came to her like it had been inside her all along, waiting to be drawn out by the proper teacher. Jemma could sense things around her before she saw them happening, like a change in the wind, a drop in temperature, or a gentle, almost indistinguishable thrumming beneath the ground she walked on.

Her training included walking barefoot through the forest, which was unpleasant for many reasons. First, because it was cold, and the rutted path wasn't a smooth surface to walk on. Jemma discovered, however, that walking barefoot and touching the trees with her fingers allowed her to feel warmth in her natural surroundings.

It feels like my touch awakens what is around me. Or maybe it is the other way around. Maybe everything I touch awakens something in me.

Her trainer's lessons about herbs, plants, and basic groundskeeping had been gentle yet instructive. Holler witch training, however, was another ball game. Walking barefoot through the forest had been Jemma's first unpleasant shock. What came after was a lot worse.

Mama B seemed to believe that painful experience was an excellent teacher. On the first day, Jemma came home bruised and scratched. A couple of days later, she had stings and burns. A week into the training, she had a rash up one side of her abdomen. She had to hide those from her father or come up with some excuse about a task she had performed at Gran's Rest.

"You're working hard," Tad remarked one day. "I hope you are enjoying your work."

Enjoyment was the last thing Jemma felt. When she

wrote in her journal, she pressed down hard and scribbled fast. Her printing wasn't very good, and her cursive was much worse, but she wrote anyway. At least, if anyone found this journal, they wouldn't be able to tell what was written in it.

> *We started with herbal magic to ward off enemies. Boo hags aren't the only thing I have to worry about, though Mama B didn't tell me what else I might face. We went into the forest to gather plants I'd never heard of. The pack Mama B gave to me had all kinds of tools in it to gather the herbs. When we got back to the cellar, Mama B had me mix every kind of herb with every other kind of herb, all the while prattling about which herb warded off what creature. I hadn't heard of the creatures, and now I don't remember all that she said.*
>
> *I tried to write them down, but she told me that if I couldn't remember them, I might as well give up. I'm damn close to giving up. We mixed that shit up for so long, I got a rash up my side, and it itches like hell. When I told Mama B about it, she told me to figure out which paste I had to make to heal it. She doesn't give me time to make pastes, though, unless they ward off the creature she's told me about that day.*

They spent a week learning how to combine herbs to make both remedies and wards. When they went back into the woods, Mama B instructed Jemma to bring the little flasks of handmade wards with her in her leather pack. The pack was heavy and made Jemma's back ache. This was a whole new level of intensive labor. Sometimes, Mama B would vanish ahead of Jemma, leaving the young woman to run up the slope into the forest, her pack bouncing on her back and creating welts in her flesh. She arrived red-faced, panting, and sweating, with the old holler witch nowhere to be seen. Jemma made sure to record her many complaints.

There's so much shit I don't know about witches: where they come from, how they came to be, who they are, how many there are. I still don't know much about Mama B. I keep asking her questions, but she either pretends she doesn't hear me or tells me, "We don't have the time. We have to train."

Despite Jemma's complaints about her lack of knowledge about witches themselves, she had to admit she was learning a lot more than she'd thought she would.

Today, Mama B introduced me to the concept of sealing. Sometimes she calls it binding instead. They're slightly different, I've learned. Sealing contains or closes off a supernatural force but allows it to move within the location it has been sealed in.

Binding is when the force cannot move either. She's told me sealing is easier, but I haven't done either yet. Sealing is done primarily through the strange markings Mama B introduced me to when she gave me the scrap of paper with the spiral design. She made me sit in front of a tree all day and carve the same marking over and over.

Jemma's back remembered every second of that tortuous task. It ached and burned. Her fingers were raw and blistered. She had band-aids wrapped around them to stop the bleeding. After she had finished, shavings from the tree lay around her, and markings stared at her from the tree. "What the hell are we keeping out?" she had asked when Mama B at last allowed her to rise and step back to examine her work.

The old woman liked not giving Jemma direct answers. "Well, if you didn't seal or bind, you'd find out, wouldn't you, dearie?"

Jemma scowled but took the answer as, "You don't want to know." Despite Mama B's less than pleasant training methods, Jemma had no choice but to trust her. The old witch knew far more than Jemma did and, as far as she could tell, always would. "I can't very well catch and kill a boo hag without learning all this," she muttered one morning after Mama B had made her hike through the forest for miles before informing her that they would be doing nothing but walking that day.

"Feel your surroundings, child. Become one with all that is around you," Mama B instructed.

Jemma frowned, grumbled something under her breath, and paid close attention. She felt the wind. She took note of its rushing sound and the leaves that rustled when it passed. Trees swayed overhead, blocking her view of the overcast sky. Jemma had the feeling this forest had been around for a very long time, even longer than Mama B. As she stood there, she felt like she was one of the trees, rooted in place for hundreds of years.

As the weeks passed, Jemma grew impatient. "When are we going to get the boo hag?"

"When you learn how to seal properly, child. The boo hag can wait until you are ready to keep it contained to one place," the old woman had answered.

Sealing can also be done with words—declarations of intent and power, as Mama B describes them, that must be believed with a sincere heart as they are clearly spoken. Of course, Mama B told me that after I spent a whole day carving symbols into a tree.

The boo hag continued to test the defenses of Jemma's home throughout the weeks of her training. "She's doing it to put you on edge and rob you of rest," Mama B explained. After considering for a long moment, during which Jemma began to feel dread, she added, "The boo hag has something wrong with her, I think."

The two of them had been sitting on a fallen tree in the forest, eating lunch. Food was a rare privilege for Jemma after her training began. Gone were the days of tea, warm bread, and preserves. Now, Mama B would pull a rabbit or squirrel from nowhere, skin it, cleanse it with some herbal concoction, and roast it over a fire. Jemma was usually so famished by the time the food was ready that she ate without complaint.

"What do you mean it has something wrong with it?" Jemma asked. As far as she could tell, the mere existence of a boo hag was wrong.

"Oh, nothing, child. Do not worry about it," Mama B replied, waving a dismissive hand.

Jemma blew out a frustrated breath. She didn't think before she muttered, "I wish I had never come up here." As soon as the words were in the air, she regretted it. Her eyes snapped up. She hoped Mama B hadn't heard her, but the hurt flickering in the old woman's eyes told her she had.

Mama B's head tilted down.

Jemma wasn't sure what to do. She had meant what she said. The training was grueling. It was not fair that she had to go through this. She'd never said she wanted to be a witch. Then again, she wouldn't have had to do it if she hadn't tried to fix a problem on her own.

Mama B shuffled past her. "Maybe it's best that we go back to the house and end your training early today."

Tad Nox was away two days for work and would not return until the following afternoon. Easter and Val, though they hadn't had any issues with the boo hag since meeting Mama B, were not available to meet Jemma for dinner at Harv's.

"I guess I'll go alone," she grumbled. She took her dad's old bike from the garage and made her way into town, refusing to remember she'd have to bike back up the mountain in the dark after she was finished. Jemma entered the diner, and eyes slid in her direction. No longer did she receive stares that said, "Who's the stranger?" A couple of people whose names she wasn't sure she knew smiled at her. She smiled back and went to the booth where she, Val, and Easter always sat.

"All alone tonight?" Holly, her waitress, asked. She had too much red lipstick on, as she always did.

Jemma opened her mouth to respond, but the sound of the door opening behind her and chattering voice distracted her. "Hey, it's New Girl," came a vaguely familiar voice. Jemma turned to see the girl with the purple streak in her hair she had met the night she'd punched AJ. The girl smiled at Jemma and sauntered over. She wasn't alone. Jemma recognized the red-haired boy from that first night.

Without invitation, the girl slid into the booth opposite Jemma and signaled for the boy to do the same. He was hesitant but did as he was asked. Holly winked at Jemma. "So, not alone?"

Jemma forced a smile. "I guess not."

"I'm Jade," the girl stated. Her eyes sparkled. She gestured at the boy with her. "This is Cameron."

"Heya," Cameron greeted.

Jemma managed a one-word response. "Hey." *What the hell am I doing? I don't know these kids,* she thought.

"We've been wondering about you," Jade remarked. "It was just our luck to find you here tonight."

Jemma's brows rose. She had the sense that these two hadn't found her by accident.

Jade leaned back. She wore an open leather jacket with a purple crop top underneath, and heavy but well-done eyeliner and a dark lip color. "You get it, don't you? It's not because you didn't grow up here, you know." Holly brought Jemma her drink, but Jade took the soda and slipped the straw between her lips. Jemma didn't know how to react, so she just sat there.

Jade continued, "You don't come to school, and you hang out with the McCarthys all the time. Oh, and you're up on the mountain. Don't you work for the—"

She was about to say "witch" but caught herself. Jemma wished for a fleeting moment that she could be normal and not have to worry about the supernatural shit she'd been learning about. She forced herself to be polite. "It's not so bad, and—"

Cameron didn't let her finish. Jade had leaned back and spoken at a normal volume, but the red-haired boy leaned forward and lowered his voice. "You know, spending time around Easter McCarthy will make ya sick." He laughed harshly.

Jade snorted, and he continued, "A lot of us heard she was fakin' her sickness for attention, and she faked it for so long it got to be real. Karma's a bitch, I guess." He laughed again as if Easter McCarthy was his favorite joke.

The thought about wanting to be normal left Jemma's mind as soon as Cameron's words were out. *They're my best friends, and I don't need anyone talking shit about them! Who does this dumbass think he is anyway, walking up to me and sitting in my booth?*

She opened her mouth to snap back, but she was interrupted again. This time, it was Jade. "We're going to a party after we eat. You should go with us." She shrugged and placed her chin in her hand. Jemma noticed her nails were painted black and her fingers bore many rings. "Get to know the other kids in town."

"Um, actually, I'm not hungry, and my dad will be wondering when I'm getting home." Jemma awkwardly got to her feet.

"It's not even dark outside yet," Cameron objected.

Jemma glanced through the window. The sun was beginning to set. The sky was an array of different shades of orange and pink. She would have enjoyed it more from the mountain. Right now, she wanted to get the hell out.

"AJ won't be there if that's what you're worried about," Jade told her to change her mind.

Cameron chuckled darkly. "Yeah, the old witch didn't

press charges for whatever the hell he did, so he's not locked up in jail, but his daddy's gonna lock him up himself."

"Groun-ded," Jaded added in a singsong voice. "I'm grounded right now, but they don't know I left the house." She chuckled, and Jemma wondered what she had done.

Jemma paused as her thoughts returned to AJ Kilmer. For a fleeting moment, she felt sorry for him. *It's not his fault he's being used by a boo hag.* She couldn't say that out loud. She was still pissed at the Kilmer boy for acting like an asshole, boo hag or no.

And these two can eat shit. I'm not putting up with this, she thought. "I've got to go," she repeated. Jemma didn't wait for another objection. She hurried toward the door but stopped at the sight of the bulletin board. The clippings and photographs from WWII were still there. This time, however, something specific caught Jemma's eye. In the center of the board was an old photograph attached via a red thumbtack. She gasped. It was the man she had seen at the edge of Mama B's forest.

"The ghost of Gran's Rest," she muttered. Mama B hadn't used any title; Jemma had come up with it since she didn't know the man's name. She reached for the photograph and turned it over. There was a name on the back, but she didn't have time to read it.

"Are ya not hungry anymore, honey?" Startled, Jemma turned to find Holly standing behind her. The waitress frowned. "Or are you suddenly hungry for history?"

Jemma's laugh sounded forced because it was. "Do you know who this is?"

Holly's frown deepened. "That stuff's boring as shit to

me." She eyed Jemma a moment longer before sighing. "Are ya gonna order or not?"

Jemma glanced beyond the waitress at the booth she had occupied only a minute before. Jade and Cameron were sitting close together, both on their phones like they had forgotten Jemma's existence. Something in her felt angry at them for it but also relieved.

Jemma forced a smile for the waitress. "Not hungry anymore." She left the diner before another word could stop her. Without anyone to talk to or anywhere else to go, Jemma decided she would ride her bike up to Gran's Rest. It couldn't be worse on her body than the rest of the intensive training she had endured over the past couple of weeks. *Maybe I can find out who that man I saw by the woods is,* she thought.

She wondered if Mama B would even want to see her after what she had said the last time she was there. She wanted to apologize. She also wanted her training not to suck so much. Jemma murmured to herself, "It's worth a try."

Mama B was not surprised to see her. It was like she sensed Jemma's arrival long before she came every time. She smiled. "Come in, my dear. I was hoping you would be by this evening." She led Jemma through the house and out the back door, then sat on the stone bench facing the downward slope and the setting sun. A cool wind blew over Jemma's skin. Relief—that was what she felt when she came here. Sometimes dread as well, but being here meant she was working toward something greater.

"Mama B," she began, turning to the old woman, "you told me we needed to be able to trust one another. I know

I've broken your trust twice and it's caused us both problems, but you're leaving me in the dark about some things. I need to know more."

Mama B gazed at the ground and the growing, dancing shadows before answering. She sighed in resignation and slipped her thin hand over Jemma's. Her touch was cold. Jemma tried not to shudder. "What do you want to know, child?"

Jemma didn't know where to begin. After thinking, she asked, "You told me there was something wrong with the boo hag. What did you mean?"

Mama B looked into the distance as if whatever lay in the sky had her answer. "A boo hag is a creature who was once a practitioner of the Art like you are becoming. A boo hag could have been a holler witch in these very mountains or some other kind of magic-user."

"There are others?" Jemma asked.

Mama B nodded but did not explain who these others were. "One who uses magic can become a boo hag when they mess with the darker, dehumanizing aspects of the Art and are filled with a terrible need to draw the vital essence from others." She gulped. "It is a vampiric existence. Even so, boo hags are still human, more or less, and can reason as we do. This one seems beyond reasoning, my child. That is why I believe there is something wrong. She is like a persistent animal, cunning but incapable or at least unwilling to either move on or come up with different strategies. From what you've told me about her prowling around your house, she does not change her methods."

Jemma nodded. Each night, if she dared to look out her window, she saw the distorted shadowy figure darting to and fro until it vanished into the night. Sometimes the shadow moved toward the road. Other times, she faded into the forest.

"Are they hurt by the sun like vampires?" Jemma asked.

Mama B's brows rose. "You have been learning, haven't you?" She shook her head. "No, boo hags can be in the sun whenever they want. That's another reason I think something is wrong with her. Her prowling only at night points to some sort of crippling either in her mind or her body."

She paused, and a far-off look came into her eyes. Jemma could have sworn tears gathered as well, but she couldn't quite tell in the growing shadows. Jemma's heart went out to the old woman. She placed a comforting hand on her arm. "What's wrong?"

"Once," Mama B began, "someone very close to me studied the Art but indulged in its darkness."

"She became a boo hag," Jemma murmured. She could sense Mama B's distress at the memory.

Mama B swallowed hard. "I had to do my worst; I had to end her. She went too far and was nothing like my old friend." She shook her head. Jemma could sense her sorrow. "I knew something was wrong with her, and this boo hag afflicting you…" Her words trailed off, and she shook her head again. She didn't need to finish her sentence. Jemma's situation reminded the old woman of one she had once been in. Jemma couldn't imagine the weight she carried.

Since the topic was emotional and sensitive, Jemma refrained from pressing her for more information. Mama B turned to face Jemma. A slight smile pulled at her lips. Jemma could see that her eyes were indeed glazed with tears. "I knew you would come back. You always do. Nothing keeps you away from what you are meant to do."

Doubt showed in Jemma's face as her brows furrowed. "Am I about to get a speech about destiny?" Jemma returned dryly. "I believe you make your fate, not that it happens to you."

Mama B chuckled. "It's a little bit of both, my dear."

Jemma waited for a speech or an explanation, but neither came. For once, she was satisfied with silence. It was companionable. Crickets buzzed as night walked in. A cold wind blew. It was almost time for Jemma to go home.

She got to her feet. "Whatever my destiny is or isn't, I know I'm meant to help the people I care about." She realized that the people she cared about included the kind, wise, fierce old woman sitting before her. Jemma smiled. "I'm going to bring that photo album back, and we're going to look through it together one of these days when we're not carving who the hell knows what into trees."

Mama B laughed. There was relief in the sound. Their relationship was once again whole.

Mama B was a little teary-eyed still but smiling. "I would love that, child."

Jemma went to her bike and made her way down the mountain in the twilight, less afraid of the encroaching darkness than she had been.

CHAPTER SEVENTEEN

Cold weather crept into Kalhoun County. Jemma had known it was coming, but she was still surprised to wake up one morning and find most of the trees leafless.

Maybe I've been in denial, she thought. She hated winter. She hated the cold. Tennessee was south of Indiana, but it didn't escape snow. With a glum expression, Jemma stared outside the living room window around midmorning.

"Going to work today?" Tad asked as he stepped out of his bedroom. "Sorry I slept in."

"That's all right." Jemma turned to her father and added a smile to her greeting. "You were tired from your travels. How was work?" She asked not because she was interested but because she didn't want to think about her tasks at Gran's Rest. Ever since her father had come back, she had been reluctant to talk about Gran's Rest or Mama B in case something slipped and she had to explain the whole damn thing.

"Ah, very good, Jem. It's going well, but this darn cold is coming in, and I can't say I like it very much." He laughed as he headed to the kitchen. "Maybe we should have moved to Florida!"

"Maybe," Jemma murmured, knowing he wouldn't hear her. She looked outside again. The sun was bright today. She remembered what Mama B had said about boo hags—that most of them had no problem prowling about in the light or the dark. The one that comes around here is afraid of the light. *There is something wrong with her*, Jemma thought.

The beep of the microwave in the next room brought Jemma's attention back to her father. Tad's head reappeared. "I'll be ready to take you up there as soon as I eat."

"That's all right," Jemma replied. "I'm not going today. Mama B needs some rest." The truth was, Jemma needed a break.

"Well then," Tad started, "maybe you wouldn't mind going into town today to pick up supplies so I can stay home and work."

Jemma smiled. "I'd love to. I can take my bike."

Tad handed her a list and some money. As he did so, he surveyed his daughter. He cocked his head, and his eyes narrowed a fraction. "Something about you has changed, Jem, and I can't put my finger on it."

Jemma stilled. What did he mean?

Her father observed her for a moment longer before putting one finger up. "Aha! You're dressed like a regular Nancy Drew! Got a magnifying glass in that pack of yours?" His eyes glittered, and he laughed. Jemma looked down at her apparel. Tad wasn't wrong. She had traded her backpack for the leather pack Mama B had given to her. She wore more practical clothes than she had before. She didn't bother with makeup or embellishing her appearance in any way before going to work. Lately, though, she had taken to applying black eyeliner.

Maybe she was going after a witchy aesthetic. Maybe she wanted to look a little more like the other girls in Solomon's Cross. Jemma didn't know. She just knew she liked it.

"You're getting more muscular too, I think," Tad commented. He wiggled his eyebrows. "You get quite the workout up there with Mama B. Does she have a gym in her cellar?"

Jemma rolled her eyes. Tad had no clue what kind of workout she was getting. "Whatever, Dad." She laughed and threw a playful punch at her father's shoulder. He feigned injury as his daughter prepared to leave the house.

Tad's shopping list reflected his personality; it was scattered and included both necessary and frivolous items. Jemma scanned the list. Milk, eggs, hot sauce, nails, paper towels, a rake, and outdoor trash bags made sense. Then there were tennis rackets (but no tennis balls), Halloween hand towels even though, as far as Jemma knew, they weren't going to celebrate Halloween, and lastly, pumpkin spice-scented hand soap. She frowned. "Dad, you don't like pumpkin spice-scented things."

Tad shrugged. "Maybe it's a part of the new Tad."

"And the tennis rackets?"

Tad made a motion as if he were whacking a tennis ball. "New hobby." He winked at his daughter. "Maybe you need to find a hobby too."

Jemma didn't have time for hobbies, not with the intensive training she was receiving, plus her school and the hours she spent worrying at night. "Okay, I'm leaving now." She chuckled. "No promises that I'll get all this stuff."

Tad smiled. "I'm sure you'll try your very best. And hey, if you see Easter or Val around, tell 'em hi for me."

Jemma turned so her father wouldn't see a change in her expression. She hadn't heard from either of the McCarthys for over a week. She knew they were busy with school, but she was getting worried. They hadn't answered her texts or calls. She had never been invited to their house, so she didn't know where they lived. She hadn't met their parents, so she couldn't find them in town if she wanted to. *I just hope they're okay,* she thought as she retrieved her bike from the side of the house and began peddling into town. Jemma figured that since she wasn't working all day at Gran's Rest, she might as well put in some physical labor somehow.

When she got to town, she found it in its normal state. Everyone she saw was talking to someone they knew as if they had known them for their whole life, which was probably true. People stared at Jemma. Some nodded and waved.

Since Jemma had a bike instead of a car, she didn't bother with tennis rackets or a rake, but she was able to find everything else. She had all the bags piled in the basket on the front of her bike when she pulled around a corner onto the main street and spied the battered truck belonging to Val McCarthy. He was walking toward it, and he was alone. Jemma had never seen him without Easter. Val glanced over his shoulder in the direction opposite Jemma. He seemed to be checking if someone was watching him.

Jemma stilled, her eyes narrowing. *What was he doing?* She decided to find out. If nothing else, she wanted to find out if he and Easter were all right. "Val!" she called as she walked her bike across the street.

Startled, he turned. Their eyes met, then for some reason, he tried to make it seem like he hadn't heard her. *What the hell?* Jemma thought, incredulous instead of relieved to see him. "Val!" she called again. He paused with his hand on the driver's side door. He had no choice but to turn around and greet her unless he wanted it to be obvious he was avoiding her.

Val turned, put his hands in his pockets, and offered Jemma a forced smile. "Jemma, how nice to see you."

Jemma's brows rose. He had never spoken so politely before. Their friendship was beyond that point, even though they'd only known one another for a month and a half. "Val, I was worried. You and Easter haven't been answering me. What's going on?"

Val shrugged. "You've been busy is all. We didn't want to bother you."

Jemma's face fell, and her voice lowered. "You could have told me."

"I know," Val answered, "and I wanted to, but..." His words trailed off.

Jemma studied him. He was acting awkward and avoiding eye contact. He looked at everything around them and never at Jemma. His hands were nonchalantly stuffed into his pockets. Jemma had the feeling he was making sure he wasn't being watched again. She didn't want to put up with his act, regardless of his reason. "Dude, what's going on?"

Her firm tone made Val's eyes meet hers at last. He swept loose strands of dark hair back from his forehead. "It's just that there's been talk."

Jemma's brows rose. "What talk?" She had a feeling it was about her and B and how much time she spent at Gran's Rest.

"Jade and Cameron have been talking shit," Val confessed at last.

"About me?" Jemma's face flushed.

Val nodded. "They say you only hang out with us so you can have shit to say when you're around your 'real friends.'" He peered at Jemma, his eyes pleading. "Is that true? Do you only hang around Easter and me so you can have stories to tell?"

Jemma couldn't believe what she was hearing. After all she'd been through for them, she deserved more trust than this. "They're lying. I never said anything like that."

"But you've been hanging out with them." Val sounded disappointed.

Jemma huffed. "I wouldn't call them inviting themselves to eat with me when I wanted to be alone 'hanging out,' and I didn't say anything about you or Easter."

Val had grown stiff and his eyes had hardened, but that went away with Jemma's reassurance. "I believe you."

Relief flooded through Jemma. "Is everything all right other than that?" she pressed.

Val nodded. Once more, he refused to look at her. "Well, kind of. I believe you, but I don't know if Easter will."

Jemma swallowed hard. "Why not?"

Val shrugged. "She's had too many mean girls become

her friend and then ditch her when it isn't fun to talk about the sick girl behind her back anymore. So now they do it in front of her, too."

Jemma wanted to throw up, then punch whoever did that to Easter. "They're all rumors, Val. I need to make her see that."

Val nodded. "Easter isn't in a good state of mind right now. She's tired. It's going to take her a little while longer."

Jemma couldn't breathe. "Is she all right? You did what Mama B said to ward off the boo hag, right?"

Val's gaze shifted farther away. "Yeah, I did."

Jemma didn't understand the problem. Wasn't Easter getting better now that the boo hag's attention was on Jemma? The thought stilled her. Maybe that was why they were avoiding her. They didn't want that creature around them, and being around her meant they were at risk.

Jemma tried to think of a way to say that out loud, but Val met her gaze once again and gave her a half-smile. "Since Easter isn't feeling well, I don't have anyone to go with to a Halloween party tomorrow. Do you wanna go with me, Jemma?"

CHAPTER EIGHTEEN

Jemma didn't know what to dress up as for Halloween and seeking her father's advice wasn't going to work. She didn't know how he would react to her going. Either he would be elated to know she was joining the social circles of her peers in some capacity, or his mind would go straight to smoking, booze, and sex, and he'd lock her up in the house all night. Jemma settled for not telling him she was going to a party and dressing as a non-slutty Nancy Drew.

"I'm hanging out with the McCarthys tonight, Tad," she told him as Val pulled up to her house in his truck.

"Be careful and have fun," Tad replied as his daughter opened the front door. It was cold and almost dark outside as Jemma sprinted to Val's truck. Twilight encroached on the property. For a second, Jemma felt a jolt of panic. For the first night in weeks, she would not be peering out her window after her father was asleep to see if a boo hag prowled around. She slid into the passenger seat, which felt strange since usually, Easter sat in this spot.

"Are you sure Easter isn't feeling well enough to come?" she asked Val.

"She's not up to socializing tonight," he told her. Jemma couldn't help but notice he avoided making eye contact, focusing instead on her costume. He chuckled nervously. "Who the hell are you?"

Jemma sighed and rolled her eyes. "I have a feeling I'm going to get asked that a lot tonight. I'm Nancy Drew." When Val stared at her, she added, "Girl detective."

Val's costume was more obvious but less original. "A vampire, yeah?" Jemma asked. She tried to sound cheerful, but she had a strange feeling. Since she'd learned that witches were real and she could train to become one, Jemma had wondered about other supernatural creatures. Surely vampires were real too. Why the hell not?

It's just a costume, Jemma told herself.

Val shrugged and pulled out of her driveway. "Last minute costume." Jemma wondered how "last minute" he meant, for the details on his cape, especially the up-turned collar, were so precise that Jemma had the notion he'd been working on this costume for a while or had at least bought it some time ago.

Last minute, huh? she repeated silently. Aloud, she asked, "So where is this party?"

Val smiled, and Jemma noticed he wore fake fangs. "You'll have to wait and find out."

What Jemma was not expecting was a journey to the other side of Solomon's Cross to the area that was most like her old suburban neighborhood in Indiana. It wasn't quite suburban, but the houses were the kind Jemma used to live in. It wasn't far from the high school Easter and Val attended. He pulled up to the largest house on the street. It was much nicer than the house Jemma had recently moved into.

The party, it appeared, was in full swing. Whoever was hosting this, their parents were out of town; that much was obvious. Blue and yellow lights flooded from the windows. Two teenage guys hauled a keg of beer up the manicured lawn. Whoever lived here had money. "This is the best place for a party," Val commented as he turned the engine off and opened his door.

Jemma had strong doubts and wondered what time the police would show up due to complaints from the neighbors. "Okay, but whose house is it?" she pushed.

Val looked away. "Oh, it's Jade's."

Jemma's brows rose. Hadn't Val just said he didn't like the kids in town who made fun of him and his sister? *Why the hell are we at this party?* Jemma wondered. She put her hand on Val's shoulder to turn him around but got distracted by a commotion in the house. Someone laughed so loud it sounded like a scream. The door burst open, and Jade stood there between two guys who looked like they were drunk.

"Valentine McCarthy, the life of the party! Come on in!" she called. She looked at Jemma but offered no greeting.

"Life of the party?" Jemma thought. It was the last description she would have assigned to Val. She remembered what Jade and Cameron had said about the McCarthys. It didn't make sense that Val had been invited. Others had drifted onto the porch. There were too many eyes on Jemma. "Well, this is going to be awkward as hell," she muttered. There was no turning back now unless she

called her father and begged him to come and pick her up. She didn't want to do that, though.

Inside the house, Jemma was battered by the scents of sweaty bodies, beer, and something that reminded her of a seaside-scented candle. When she moved farther into the house, the scents of cigarettes and weed overpowered everything else. Stares drilled into her. Whatever these kids were thinking, it was clear that they had not expected her, of all people, to show up. Jemma glanced at Val and nudged him with her elbow. "Didn't think this was your kind of scene."

"Well," Val answered, forcing a smile, "maybe I wanted a change for once." He grabbed a red plastic cup and drew beer from the keg. "You want one?"

Jemma wrinkled her nose.

Val tipped his cup back, and his words were muffled before he drank. "Suit yourself, party pooper." Jemma had been called worse and by people closer to her, but it stung coming from Val. *Why did you want me to come to this with you?* she wanted to ask. Val, however, was quite distracted.

They moved into the living room, where the stereo thumped so loud, Jemma felt the beat in every part of her body. Val's eyes were wide and full of excitement. *Geez, he's actually having fun,* Jemma realized. The farther in they went, the more people eyed them. The stares continued to follow Jemma, but no one spoke a word to her. Others greeted Val and even leaned close to murmur to him while glancing over his shoulder at Jemma.

"What the hell is going on?" Jemma demanded as they stepped into the kitchen. "Didn't think this was your kind of party." She stopped at the sight of a couple making out by the sink. She groaned and turned to face Val.

Val shrugged. "Did you hear what that guy said?" He winked. "You've got a reputation around here, Jemma Nox."

Her brows rose. "Because I punched AJ?"

Val drank. "Among other things." His eyes roved back and forth, drinking everything in. Jemma rolled her eyes. It was obvious Val had never been to anything like this. Jemma, on the other hand, had been to a couple of high school parties, mainly to rebel against her mother. She didn't feel a need to be at one now, especially since she didn't know anyone here. "Wanna dance?" Val asked, oblivious to Jemma's discomfort. He had only drunk one cup of beer, but his eyes were already glazed.

Great, Jemma thought. *Not only did I come to a party I don't want to be at, but I also came with a lightweight.* The last thing she wanted to do was drive his truck to her house. Also, what would her father think of her bringing a boy home who was too drunk to drive his truck? Aloud, she asked, "Does everyone hate AJ that much?"

Val shrugged. "Yeah, pretty much. It wasn't always like that. He used to be pretty cool." He stared into his empty cup as if it were showing him memories.

Jemma was curious and didn't care who heard her. "What happened to make everyone hate him so much?"

Val's eyes flicked up, and his expression hardened. "Why do you want to know?" His voice was soft, but there was a dangerous edge to it.

There were many reasons she wanted to know. AJ had commented about his father needing money, but the young man owned an expensive sports car. He seemed to take care of his most prized possession but couldn't keep anything else together. "Everybody says he changed when his mom died."

Val nodded. "It's true. When his mom died, it was like he broke. She was rich, too. It was her that held the family together."

"Really?" Jemma asked.

"Yeah," Val responded. "When she died, she left a good chunk of change to each of her kids. AJ used his share to buy that damn car."

Jemma didn't miss the jealousy in Val's voice.

Val continued. "I think he hated his mom, though. Everybody always said she had secrets, especially about her money."

"What kind of secrets?" Jemma asked.

Val, however, was looking for another drink. Either he didn't hear her question or ignored it.

Jemma stared at him. "I haven't known you that long, Val, but I don't think this is like you."

A voice behind her interrupted her, "Val, what are you doing here?" The voice trembled.

Jemma turned, and her eyes went wide. Standing behind her was Easter, dressed in black and without a costume. Her eyes welled with tears. Jemma's eyes wrenched back to Val. The younger McCarthy was shocked to see his sister. "Easter, what are you doing here?"

Easter's face and tone were angry when she responded. "I asked you! I came looking for you because I didn't know where you had gone, and someone said you came here, and…" Her words trailed off as she noticed Jemma standing between them. Hurt flickered across her expression. She looked at her brother. "So, that's how it is? The two of you just go to parties and leave me at home now?"

"What? No!" Jemma objected. "Val told me you didn't feel well enough tonight."

Easter started crying, not worried about who might be watching. Val tried to explain, but Jemma didn't hear whatever he had to say over the red-hot rage in her head. She turned on him. "What the hell? You lied to me! No one invited you until you told them you would bring me, did they? You're using my reputation, which, by the way, I don't give a shit about!"

Jemma had never gone off on anyone like this except for one time when she'd had an explosive fight with her mother. It was a memory she had worked hard to forget. Now, standing in front of Val, she felt that same anger welling up.

Val's head dropped. Easter ran out of the house, face down so no one would see her crying. How she had gotten there, Jemma didn't know. Had she walked by herself? The thought made Jemma sick with guilt. *I should have called her!*

She ran after her, calling her name and pushing through the beery, sweaty bodies. Someone tripped her, and she sprawled on the hardwood floor. She hit it with a heavy *thwack* and groaned at the impact. Laughter rose behind her. Jemma struggled to her feet, caught between wanting to catch up to Easter, sit with her pain until it went away, and go find Val and strangle him.

By the time she got to her feet, Easter had disappeared. Val, however, was behind Jemma. "Shit, shit, shit," she hissed. This night was getting worse, and she had a feeling it wasn't over.

"Jem, I'm so sorry. I don't know why I—" Val started.

Eyes flashing, Jemma got in his face. She didn't care who was looking at them. "You *do* know why and you're going to tell me right now!"

Val stared at her, then grabbed her arm and led her down the hall. He opened the bathroom door. The small room smelled like smoke and steam, as if the shower had just been turned off. "Hurry up," Jemma growled.

Val looked at the tiled floor for a few seconds, then met Jemma's gaze. "It's just that ever since Easter got sick, all I've been is the guy whose sister is sick. I wanted to get away for a night and be myself."

"Drinking cheap beer in a vampire costume is who you are?"

The reality of the situation dawned on Val.

"And what about me?" Jemma demanded. "Why did you bring me?" Val didn't answer, but Jemma was able to figure it out. "Was it because of my reputation? Was bringing me going to get you some attention?"

Val's eyes welled with tears. Jemma decided she should cease her tirade. Her features and voice softened. "I don't understand how ditching your sister and going to a party where there are people you don't even like makes you your own person." She put her hands on his shoulders and made him look at her. "You are already your own person, Valentine McCarthy. Remember that."

A tear slipped down his white cheek. "You're the only one who sees it that way, Jemma Nox."

Jemma's heart ached for him. She stepped back and

leaned against the bathroom wall, giving Val a moment to collect himself.

At last, he added, "I didn't want to become like him. Like AJ."

"You're nothing like him," Jemma murmured.

Val hung his head. "We used to be best friends, you know."

Jemma wasn't sure if she had misheard him. "You and AJ. Best friends." There was little in the world that was harder to imagine.

Val nodded. "We were best friends when we were kids. Then Easter got sick, and he had problems with his mom. His sisters moved away, and the problems got worse. Then, one day, it was like he snapped." Val's gaze was far away. "He started making fun of Easter and wanted me to say things like that too."

He shook his head. "I couldn't, not even for him. Then his mom died. He bought that stupid car and got angry with me over stupid things. He blamed me for a scratch on his car and a little bit of food on the seat. He came unhinged, Jemma." Val's eyes met hers, and he shrugged. "So, we ain't friends anymore."

Jemma couldn't breathe, but she wasn't sure how much of it had to do with Val's revelation and how much had to do with the heavy smoke in the house. Jemma opened her mouth to say something, but a shriek wrenched her attention elsewhere. Val opened the bathroom door. In the living room, a girl stood in a ring of other teens. At first, she appeared to be drunk, but the longer Jemma watched her, the more uneasy she became.

She made weird sobbing sounds and staggered around.

The faces of the kids around the girl told Jemma one thing: this wasn't regular drunken revelry. There was something off about this girl's actions. Val's face went paler than normal. He looked like he was about to throw up. "That's Jade. She never acts like that."

"Shit!" Jemma hissed. She hadn't recognized the girl as the one hosting the party. Something had changed about her, and she had a really bad feeling about it. "Fuck!"

"What is it?" Val turned to look at her. He was terrified.

Jemma swallowed hard. Since learning the reason for Easter's affliction, Jemma had mostly stayed in places where there were wards, like at home and at Gran's Rest. Anytime she went into town, something bad happened. Now she was at a party where the hostess wasn't acting like herself. "I think the boo hag followed me here, Val."

Val's terror increased. This place wasn't warded. Jemma was out in the open, and it was dark. What was to stop the creature from trying to hurt her? He gripped Jemma's arm with a shaking hand. She turned toward the door. "We have to go."

We have to get to Mama B and tell her we need to move fast.

CHAPTER NINETEEN

Jemma wasn't sure which was more illegal: driving a vehicle without a driver's license up a winding mountain road at night or allowing her intoxicated friend to do it. Even if Val had been sober, he was too overwhelmed and dazed by his sister's sudden appearance to form thoughts. Jemma's hands shook as she placed the key in the ignition.

I have to get the damn boo hag away from here, she thought, breathing heavily. Jemma had driven a car a few times before but never a vehicle as large as a truck and never up a mountain. She gripped the steering wheel like she was holding on for dear life and hoped no one was watching as she attempted to pull off the street.

Val just looked out the window, pale and terrified. Did he realize they were in the truck or where they were going?

A hundred other thoughts raced through Jemma's mind. Easter was upset with her and Val, and it was up to Jemma to fix it. Her father didn't know where she was and would be calling in an hour or so. Val had lied to her. A boo hag had followed her to a party. Jemma didn't like Jade very much, but she didn't want anything supernatural to go after anyone else if she could prevent it. Jemma weighed her thoughts to figure out what needed to be addressed first.

What she knew for sure was that she needed to get to Mama B as soon as she could.

The truck rattled up the rutted roads, sounding like it was going to break down at any second. Every time Jemma hit a pothole, a spike of panic went through her since she thought she was going to spin off the road. Val didn't notice her distress.

The trip up the mountain lasted an eternity. The road seemed never-ending, every turn and bend looking the same as the last. She was certain she was going in circles. At long last, the top of the hill came into view. Jemma breathed a sigh of relief. She had never been happier to see Mama B's house.

The house was dark except for one window filled with light on the right side of the house where the parlor was. Jemma guessed Mama B was sitting in front of the fire, enjoying the night while she could—or perhaps waiting for the two teens who had come to ruin it. Val sat in the passenger seat, still in a daze. "Come on, get out of the car!" Jemma hissed. Val snapped back to his senses, swallowed hard, and did as Jemma commanded.

Mama B opened the door before they knocked, having sensed their arrival. She looked at Jemma but didn't say a word. Then she looked at Val and frowned. "Real vampires don't look like that."

Val shifted uncomfortably, but Mama B's next words

made him even more uncomfortable. "And where on earth is Easter?" Jemma thought Mama B knew at least some of the answer to her question. Jemma thought Mama B wanted Val to answer since she looked at the young man instead of at Jemma.

Val's face flushed. His eyes welled with tears. "I don't know." His expression was stricken with worry, and terror still hung behind his dark eyes.

"Mama B, we came because something bad happened at this party we were at. I think the boo hag followed me," Jemma wailed.

Mama B's eyes went wide. She swallowed hard and beckoned the two teenagers into her house. "Out on Halloween while a boo hag is following you? What were you thinking?"

Jemma's heart sank. Mama B was right. She should have thought about that. She had a feeling Halloween meant something different to the old witch than costumes and candy.

As Jemma had expected, a fire was burning in the hearth. Mama B gave them tea and told them to sit on the sofa opposite her rocking chair. The old woman remained standing as Jemma told the story about Jade and the moment when she seemed possessed. Jemma's hands shook as she attempted to hold her teacup steady. Val's cup also rattled against his saucer.

"Easter left before that?" Mama B asked at last, concern etched into her face.

Jemma and Val looked at each other. They hadn't said anything about Easter coming to the party. Either Mama B knew something with her supernatural ability, or she assumed Val never went anywhere without his sister. "We think so," Jemma responded, "but we don't know for sure. I lost sight of her."

Mama B shook her head in either distress or disappointment. Jemma couldn't tell which.

"I knew I had to leave," Jemma added desperately. "I didn't want that thing tormenting anyone else. I should have known it would follow me. It was stupid of me to go anywhere there weren't wards."

"Child, calm down," Mama B interjected gently. "You did the right thing by leaving, but I am afraid we are running out of time more quickly than I anticipated. Do you remember when I told you there might be something wrong with this particular boo hag?"

Jemma nodded. It was the last thing she'd forget.

Mama B sighed. "Well, it is stranger still that the creature would put herself in a situation like a party where there are so many people around. Her actions are growing more aggressive."

Jemma gulped. Her training had been going on for weeks. In recent days, Mama B had begun praising her for her progress instead of admonishing her. She was improving, but… "I don't feel ready," she murmured.

Mama B laid a warm hand on Jemma's shoulder. "Sometimes, my dear, *I* don't feel ready, and I've been doing this for a very long time."

Jemma knew she was supposed to be comforted by Mama B's words, to feel less alone, but they made her feel worse. "At least what I've seen tonight shows me more of what I'm up against." She gave a deep sigh. She could no longer be consumed with worry over how things would turn out. "What do we need to do?"

Mama B's face hardened as her thoughts returned to the boo hag. "We will need to trap her so we can try to bind her. You've been doing well with your bindings, Jemma. I believe you can do it, but you mustn't. You are right. You are not ready for this."

Jemma deflated, but she was also relieved. This meant Mama B would have to do the magical work. "What will this do to the boo hag?" she asked. The fate of the creature had never been discussed. Killing it seemed like the best thing, but Jemma remembered what Mama B had said about the boo hags being humans who had gone too far in the Art. That meant it could come back if nourished well enough.

Mama B was slower to answer this time. Jemma got worried as the old woman's eyes traveled about the room. "Binding the creature with my power means my power will have to overcome hers, thus destroying one or the other. The creature is weak. We know this because she cannot penetrate simple wards."

"Destroying one or the other," Jemma echoed. The words were heavy. Either Mama B would be overcome by the boo hag, or more likely, she would live, but the creature would not be given a chance to come back from the darkness of the Art. Jemma's lips trembled. "I want to help. I've been binding well. I can…"

Her words trailed off as Mama B gave her a kind but sad smile. "You most of all, child, should not try to bind her alone since you haven't had much practice."

Jemma's eyes welled. "What do you mean?"

Mama B sank into her rocking chair at last and folded her thin hands in her lap. "Binding the creature will release its power, but that power will need somewhere else to go. It will seek to consume the person who binds the creature. The boo hag's magic will be dark and all-consuming and difficult to combat. Someone with experience and practice will have to go up against it."

Jemma's hands trembled on her teacup. "Does it have to be that way?"

Mama B nodded and stared at her own hands as if years of her magic were written there.

Jemma thought about everything that had led to this point, and Easter's face came into her mind. *Easter believes I don't want anything to do with her. I need to prove her wrong.* Jemma looked at Mama B and made a choice. It might be stupid and reckless, but she felt it was necessary. Jemma didn't want Easter to die from her sickness.

She did not tell Mama B or Val about her choice. She didn't even form the words for it in her mind. She felt it deep within her. She knew what she had to do.

Mama B's gaze had gone far away. "It's been this way before." She murmured the words in so low a tone that Jemma almost couldn't tell what she was saying. She had a feeling Mama B was talking about the woman she had been close to who had become a boo hag. Had she tried to bind the boo hag and by some miracle, survived it? Jemma saw that as the only possibility.

Mama B looked up. "Holler witches have been dealing with boo hags in these mountains since we came here." She sat back and told more of the story. Jemma and Val listened in fascination. Gradually, Jemma's hands stopped shaking. Her tears went away, and at last, she was able to drink her warm, soothing tea. The beverage helped her feel at ease.

Mama B started by explaining that the holler witches had come to the Appalachian Mountains from different parts of the world at different times. Jemma remembered the journal pages in her house detailing travels from Eastern Europe to Tennessee shortly after World War II. Once the holler witches moved to the mountains, they became vital to the lives of people who could not travel to hospitals. They became midwives and experts in all herbal remedies, curing many illnesses.

Mama B's eyes filled with a dark memory. "We were left in peace to perform our work, but not all of the people liked what we were doing. The town elders claimed our practices were evil despite their lack of proof for their claims."

"The elders?" Val asked. "I've never heard of them."

Jemma hadn't either, but that made sense since she had been in this area for far less time.

Mama B nodded. "There were seven elders who made laws and enforced them. They were the heads of the seven main families in the communities." She looked at Val. "The McCarthys were among them, of course."

Val's face somehow became paler.

"Eventually, there came a time when enough people believed the elders and they all came against us, decreeing we halt our work and repent before God lest they drive us from the mountains with hellfire." She chuckled darkly. "That sounds a lot more like evil than herbs and delivering babies, doesn't it?"

Jemma nodded. Val leaned close to his friend. "Have you ever been in the old church in Solomon's Cross?" Jemma shook her head. Even from afar, the old white church at the far end of town had given her the creeps. "If there's anything haunted around here, it's that place," Val finished.

Mama B seemed to agree. "The elders used God and their holy books to make their case."

"But it didn't work," Jemma responded.

Mama B's eyes were grave. "It didn't. We stood against them. The elders of the town left one by one without their families. As they departed, it was like a shadow was lifted from the mountains."

Jemma wondered what the elders' leaving had entailed, but she supposed the story would go on for quite some time if Mama B gave all the details.

The old woman shared one last thing. "The Book of Solomon was left behind, and with it many answers to many mysteries." She leaned forward. "You see, the town was named Solomon's Cross, but no one knew why. Town names always have a long and deep history behind them."

Jemma's brows furrowed. Mama B talked about the book as if everyone knew about it. Seeing Jemma's confused expression, the old woman explained. "In ancient Israel, there was a king named Solomon who was the wisest and wealthiest king in the world. There was a book attributed to him a thousand years after his death containing spells that could summon demons. It is the oldest of all the magical texts, and somehow, the elders of this town gained possession of it."

Jemma's eyes went wide, and her heart hammered. "Where is it now?"

"I don't know." Mama B sounded sorrowful. "We only saw it once. Only touched its gold cover once before it disappeared. Where it went is still a mystery to me today."

The Case of the Missing Spell Book sounded like a Nancy Drew book to Jemma. She was intrigued by this revelation about the past of Solomon's Cross, but there was far more to be concerned about at the moment.

"Do you know what all this means?" Mama B asked.

Val nodded. "It means the town elders were using magic to summon demons. They were bringing evil into the mountains, but they had to blame it on someone."

Mama B nodded. "So, they blamed it on the women with the herbs and the babies." She laughed harshly. "That happened in King Solomon's day, too."

These stories, old as they were, added nothing new. Jemma was saddened.

Mama B went on. "The stain of what the elders claimed about the holler witches remained as well. It was never washed away. From those days on, we were seen with fear by some people." Mama B gave Jemma and Val a sad smile. "But not everyone." She reached for Jemma's hand. "It is time for you to find your friend. We have work to do."

When Jemma and Val stepped outside, there was a tense silence between them. Val stared at the ground as Jemma collected her thoughts. The plan was to go home to get a good night's rest and hope Easter was there.

"Jemma, I'm sorry," Val said at last. Jemma glanced at him. She could see the sincerity of his apology in his face. "We have to find Easter so we can fix this."

Jemma still felt like punching Val, but she had to set her wrath aside for the time being so they could focus on Easter and the boo hag. "Are you sober enough to drive back home?"

Val nodded, and Jemma tossed him the keys.

CHAPTER TWENTY

Jemma texted Easter the next morning, pleading with her to meet so they could talk. To Jemma's immense surprise and relief, the older McCarthy sibling responded.

I'll be at Harv's in an hour.

Jemma hurried down the mountain on her bike. Her father was sleeping in since he had the day off work, so he could not drive her. Jemma wasn't mad. She wasn't ready to explain the problems between her and her friends. The ride was cold since even though the sun was out, the wind was swift and biting. When Jemma parked her bike outside Harv's diner, she was windburned and shivering.

Easter was inside. Jemma spied her through the window. She was alone. Jemma was relieved since she wasn't quite yet ready to repair things with Val. He had apologized, but Jemma had a feeling there was more to the situation. *We can't spend too much time in town,* Jemma thought. *I don't want the boo hag following me here.* She wasn't as anxious about it since it was daytime, but she remembered what Mama B had said about the creature: the boo hag was getting more aggressive toward Jemma and anyone she was around. They had to move quickly, and it all started with Jemma making amends with Easter.

Easter wore her beanie and black clothes as usual. She nodded at Jemma in greeting when she entered. Jemma's eyes trailed over the midmorning patrons, mostly truckers stopping for brunch or men having business meetings outside their offices.

As soon as they were seated, the waitress named Barb, who Jemma met her first night here, gave them a look with raised brows as if to say, "Aren't you both supposed to be in school?" Jemma hadn't thought about that. Since she was homeschooling, she had the flexibility to come into town when she wished. Easter, however, was skipping school. The girl somehow knew that was on Jemma's mind. Her eyes watched the table. "I'm not going to school today." She shrugged. "I told my parents I didn't feel well and that I was going to go get some soup."

There were a hundred reasons Easter might not be going, but Jemma guessed it had everything to do with Val and the party the night before. Jemma reached across the table and took her hand. The other girl did not draw it away. Instead, she looked at Jemma. Her eyes were full of emotion but not tears. "I was hurt when I saw you and Val last night, Jemma. I thought that since you've been so busy lately, you didn't care about me anymore."

Jemma's heart sank. "I've been with Mama B at Gran's Rest, training." She didn't add "to be a witch" since there were many ears around and she didn't know how many of the diner's patrons were listening to their conversation. "I've been distracted, I will admit." Then there was the matter of the rumors. Jemma had to clear those up too.

Easter allowed her to explain, and a relieved smile appeared. "I believe you, Jemma, and I'm sorry I didn't seek you out when I heard the rumor."

Jemma shrugged. "It's okay. I'm betting nastier rumors have been spread."

Easter laughed harshly, then her features softened. "I'm confused about Val, though. He'd never do anything like that to me, but he did. I don't know what's happened." She leaned close to Jemma. "Do you think there's any way the boo hag has turned on him?"

Jemma's eyes widened, but she shook her head. "I've seen it prowling around my house too often. I don't think it's had the time to go after Val."

Jemma remembered what Val had told her in the bathroom at the party—how he wanted to be his own person, apart from his sister. Then she recalled what she had learned about AJ Kilmer. She brought that up. "Val told me he and AJ used to be friends. Were you friends with AJ too?"

Easter's expression hardened, then she slumped. They were interrupted the next moment by Barb's approach. Once their order had been taken, she moved off, and Easter answered Jemma's question. "Friends, yes. Something more? Maybe. I don't know." She shook her head, looking dejected.

"Something more" clanged around in Jemma's skull. Had Easter and AJ liked each other?

"It doesn't matter now," Easter said with a sigh. "He

became as 'bad boy' as he could get, and it was a stupid, childish crush anyway. But he and Val were close, and it hurt Val like hell when AJ started acting like an asshole."

Jemma could tell there were layers to this story, but Easter wasn't in any mental condition to peel them back. She related to Easter what Mama B had said the night before but left out the part where the witch who would bind the boo hag would also face death. "If you're off school for the day, we can go up to Gran's Rest together. My dad can give us a ride. Mama B needs help to prepare."

Easter smiled, and for the first time in weeks, she looked happy. "I would love that."

When Jemma and Easter arrived at Gran's Rest, Mama B gave them a broad smile. She did not ask where Val was or why Easter wasn't in school. Whatever she might have wondered, she found her own answers. "Lovely to have you both here. Let's get to work."

Jemma was relieved to discover they would be spending the day collecting herbs to use to catch the boo hag instead of training in the forest. The work would be much easier on both her mind and her body. "We'll need every kind of brew a boo hag would be attracted to or curious about," Mama B told them.

"How do we know what a boo hag will want to come up and sniff?" Jemma asked.

Mama B wagged a finger. "Ah, I forget you do not know what we're dealing with, child. It is high time you read books on the creatures we're hunting and binding. I'll go get one from my library."

Jemma and Easter exchanged looks, curious about her library. Jemma hadn't known the old woman had books, but then again, there were two floors in the house she had never seen. *With a lot more mysteries,* she supposed. The paintings with the painted-out eyes came into her mind.

Mama B laughed at their expressions. "Someday, girls, I will show you my library, but for today, one book only."

While she was gone, which was for some time, Jemma and Easter continued to procure the herbs from Mama B's list. Jemma noticed a change within her friend. Easter had been sick for a very long time, and even though she was better every day, it was a slow process. Still, she seemed to have more energy. She took few breaks, and color bloomed in her cheeks. She seemed happy with her work, smiling now and then instead of needing to lie down on the grass. The sun shone overhead, but Jemma knew the warm autumn weather would not last long. It was the first week of November; the temperatures would drop very soon.

When Mama B reappeared, she had something in her hands. Jemma and Easter peered at the ancient-looking tome, which had faded gold lettering in a language Jemma did not know. The inside, however, was written in English. Jemma scanned the first page and noted two things, both of which struck her as familiar. The language of the content was English, but it included many terms she did not recognize or understand. The handwriting was very similar to the handwriting in the journal at her house, though it was far less cramped and messy. The writer of this book had taken her time. These were not the scattered, often emotional thoughts that filled the pages of the woman's journal.

Easter was captivated by the book. She turned to the second page. "Can I read this for a little bit?" she asked Mama B with a pleading expression.

The old witch chuckled. "Do as you please, dearie. You never know what reading can do to revive the spirit until you've found a book to capture your soul."

Jemma wasn't sure about that. She had never liked reading for fun, but there was no doubt Easter's interest and joy grew the moment she opened the book. Easter curled up on the porch swing, and Jemma joined Mama B to complete their herb gathering tasks.

The old woman glanced at Easter and leaned close to Jemma. "I see potential in that girl when it comes to the Art. She could become a witch herself when she isn't as frail."

Jemma did not try to hide her surprise. It was difficult to imagine Easter in the kind of training Jemma had been subjected to over the past weeks. Holler witch training was no sinecure. Jemma had almost given up. Then she remembered how fast Easter had caught onto Mama B's instruction. Now she was reading a book on boo hags and whatever else with avid interest. Mama B murmured, "Only time will tell us what is left of the sweet girl after what the damned creature did to her."

Jemma changed the subject. "When will we try to catch it?" She didn't like saying "boo hag" out loud when she could avoid it. She felt like it followed her everywhere, even though Mama B had wards up around her house.

Mama B considered, then asked, "When does your father leave town for work again?"

"This weekend, I believe," Jemma answered. It made sense. They would need to trap the boo hag at Jemma's house since that was where the creature prowled at night. She preferred that Tad not be around for that.

The reality of what they needed to do hit her full force, and she froze. "Are you all right, child?" Mama B asked. Jemma turned to find the old woman's face creased with worry. She nodded but couldn't find the words to reassure her mentor. Mama B sighed. "Fret not, my dear. It will all be okay in the end. You must trust me."

Jemma had no reason to believe it was true, not with the choice she was determined to make. "This weekend is when we'll do it," she agreed. Yet again, she would be hiding something from her father, which made her unhappy. *It will be done soon,* she thought, *and what I've hidden or not hidden won't matter anymore.*

"Shit, I have to get home," Jemma muttered as she looked at her watch. It was nearly 11:00; time had passed quickly. Mama B had invited her and Easter to stay for dinner. Upon calling their parents, they had received permission. Following dinner, the three women had gone into the cellar, and while separating and storing herbs, they'd had a lively conversation and forgotten about the concept of time.

"Shit, me too," Easter responded. "My parents will be worried sick. I'm calling Val right now to come pick us up."

Jemma dreaded having to see him but didn't want to call her father. She wondered why he hadn't called her yet. Feeling nervous, she finished her task and told Mama B goodnight.

Ten minutes later, Val pulled up, and the girls hopped in. Easter had had a marvelous day and was eager to share the details with Val even after what he had done to her. Jemma, however, sat in stony silence in the back seat. When they got to her house, she ignored Val and told Easter goodnight. "I'll see you this weekend, if not before!"

Jemma made her way into the house, which was dark except for the kitchen. Once inside, she heard her father shifting in his chair at the kitchen table. When she entered, on the edge of curfew, she found him bent over the table, hand on his chin. He wore an expression of concern mixed with distress and undertones of anger. "What's wrong?" Jemma began, and her father looked up.

"Where have you been this evening, Jemma?"

"At Mama B's, like I said," Jemma answered. She set her leather pack on the table. Tad gave it a rueful look, no doubt wondering why she had replaced her backpack with something less suitable. Jemma explained that they had lost track of time.

Tad frowned. "When did you find the time to do your homework today?"

Jemma stilled. She had forgotten about an assignment due today. "Shit," she muttered.

Tad didn't rebuke her for her language, but he did lean back and sigh with his face toward the ceiling. He dragged a heavy hand through his hair. Tad Nox was Jemma's friend, but he was her father first. He was not her friend at this moment. She realized that and braced herself.

"Look, Jem," he started, "I know your grades have been slipping, and while I appreciate you making money at Gran's Rest, learning should be your number one priority. Remember the agreement we made when I told you you didn't have to go to school?"

Jemma nodded, ashamed and defeated. With everything going on, her chemistry test had been the last thing on her mind, and turning in herbs for luring boo hags wasn't a good idea as a replacement.

Tad sighed again, looking at his daughter with earnest concern. "I have to leave tomorrow for the next five days, but I don't think I should."

Jemma's heart sank. "Why not?" If her father didn't leave, they couldn't carry out their plan.

"If I stay, I can help you get back on track."

Indignation swelled within her. *I don't need your help,* she wanted to snap, but seeing her father's distress, she didn't want to cause any more damage.

"There's another thing," Tad continued. "I feel like you keep secrets from me. I know you and Val went to a party the other night. I don't care about that, but I wish you had told me the truth."

"Dad, I'm sorry," Jemma started, but her words were cut off as her father moved some of her homework off the table and revealed to her what lay behind it. Jemma's heart dropped to her toes. Fuck was the only word clanging around in her head as her eyes fell on the box of mementos she had been hiding in her closet. She scrambled for an excuse. "Dad, I—" She couldn't think of what to say, and it didn't seem like Tad wanted to hear it anyway.

"I received a notice about another assignment you had failed to turn in, Jem, so I went to your room to see if I could find it." He shrugged. "I was hoping you had finished it and I could submit it for you to help you out, but I found something else instead. I smelled something odd coming from your closet. When I opened it, I found some herbs. That's a whole other thing you're going to have to explain, but it was the false back I noticed more." He gestured at the box of mementos. "It's not even that you hid it from me, Jem. It's that when I asked if you knew where they were, you lied to me."

Tad swallowed hard. "I'm concerned about the change in your behavior, Jemma." He replaced her nickname with her full name, drawing her attention closer. "Maybe if you had a mother around, it would help."

Jemma didn't want to hear the word "mother." "You wanna talk about lies, Dad? Fine." Her anger swelled up, and she couldn't put the flames out. "You lied first when you said you were going to move on but still kept all this shit around that reminds us of the woman who ruined our life!"

Tad's face fell. Hurt flickered in his eyes. "I'm the parent, Jemma. I get to make the call on what is best."

Jemma couldn't help herself. She stood up quickly, face red. She didn't hide a single emotion. "Fine! If you're the adult, then you should start acting like it and see that holding on to your ex-wife is destroying you and hurting me! I was the one pulling the weight the first year after she left. I did all the shit that needed to be done for both of us."

It was the truth, but as soon as the words were out, Jemma wished she had found a better, more loving way of saying it.

Tad sank back against his chair, stunned. They had never gotten into it like this. Each had had their fair share of fights with Delilah but never with one another. Jemma waited in tense silence as her father stared straight ahead, lost in thought and feelings. Memories of fights they didn't want to remember plagued them. At last, Tad spoke to his daughter one last time for the night. His voice was low and stiff. "Go to your room, Jemma. I'll be doing some serious reconsidering about our lives here and what it's going to look like moving forward."

Dread curled in Jemma's stomach. The last thing she wanted was to have to go to Solomon's Cross High, but none of it would matter if there was still a boo hag stalking her. *He doesn't know about all the shit I'm dealing with right now,* Jemma thought. *It's not normal teenage girl shit, either. I know none of it is his fault, but he wouldn't believe me if I told him.*

Tad stood up, hands in his pockets, and looked his daughter in the eyes. "I won't be leaving for work because I've learned I can't trust you." Of all the things he had said so far, this one hurt the most. Jemma felt like she had been pierced in the heart. The last thing she wanted to lose was her father's trust. *But I can't tell him. I can't tell him what I'm going to do.*

Angry and scrambling for words, Jemma tried to figure out how they were going to carry out their plan to trap the boo hag with her father staying at home. Her only chance had slipped through her fingers. *I can't be hounded by that damn creature until he decides he can trust me again,* Jemma thought.

"Go to your room, Jemma," Tad repeated. She had no choice but to obey. She went to the loft, spied the journal pages on her bed, and wondered if he had gone through those too. *None of this would have happened if you hadn't decided this was the one place in the world you wanted to move to,* Jemma thought.

She slipped between the blankets but did not sleep for a long time, even after she heard her father snoring in the bedroom below.

CHAPTER TWENTY-ONE

Jemma awoke the next morning, knowing she would have to come up with a new plan. *I'm not going to let him stop me,* she thought as her father's hurt-filled face from the night before filled her mind. *I can't tell him the truth. Not yet.* That meant she only had one option left: look through the journals for a solution to her problem. It had given her an answer before, though not a very helpful one.

Help me better this time, she thought as she searched the pages.

The pieces seemed more scattered than ever. She set to sorting them into categories: daily entries, recipes for brews and concoctions, and content she couldn't distinguish. Sketches of plants alerted Jemma to pages with recipes on them. At long last, she found a page titled *Sleeping Draughts*. The ingredients were easy to read, but the instructions were so cramped that Jemma was tempted to crumple the paper and throw it in a trash can. This was far worse than any chemistry test.

Fuming in frustration, she decided on the first sleeping draught listed. The problem was in making it while her father wasn't looking. Tad had ordered her to stay home for the rest of the week via a note left for her on the kitchen table before he went into town. She would not go to work until she was caught up on her assignments and her online teachers were satisfied with her progress. "Time to call in the reinforcements." Groaning, Jemma dialed Easter's number.

The girl arrived after school, ready to help. Tad had spent the day in town and had been gone long enough to make Jemma worry. *He's upset with me, and now he's hiding,* she thought. *So much for not trusting me and needing to keep me in his sight.*

When Tad arrived home at last, the sun was setting, and Jemma was hungry. Hearing voices in the kitchen, he went there first. He was frowning when he stepped in, but the frown faded into confusion at the sight of Easter.

"Easter's come to study with me, Dad. I hope that's all right," Jemma explained stiffly. Tad gave her a curt nod before going to his bedroom. Jemma had given Easter a vague reason for why she needed her to brew the sleeping draught, but Easter had read between the lines. While Tad was in his room, she slipped the draught into Jemma's backpack and leaned close.

"I followed the directions you gave me. When are we doing this?"

"Tomorrow night," Jemma answered. Dread rose within her. That was so close. She held her pencil firmly to the paper where she was scribbling notes for her missed test.

One second, she was a normal teenager studying with her friend and having a fight with her dad. The next, she was planning to put her father to sleep so she could catch a boo hag in her backyard with an immortal witch. *All in the day of a teenage witch,* she thought ruefully.

Sabrina and Nancy Drew hadn't done enough to prepare her for this.

It wasn't all bad. Tad had managed some degree of cheerfulness due to Easter's presence. He ordered the girls pizza and left them unbothered until they were finished studying. "Val's here," Easter announced at around eight o'clock. "I'll see you tomorrow, Jemma."

Tad, hearing her from the living room, asked, "Tomorrow?"

"We're going to study again," Jemma explained.

Tad stared at the two of them for a moment. "I think it would be best if Jemma studied alone so she can focus. We'll see you another day, Easter."

Easter gave Jemma a long look before she went to the truck parked in the driveway. Indignation swelled within Jemma. Being grounded was one thing but being isolated was a different matter. Jemma followed Easter to the door and watched as she met Val at the truck. When she turned back, she expected some remark from her father or another fight to ensue, but his recliner was empty, and he was nowhere to be found.

"Hiding again, eh?" Jemma muttered as she went back to her homework.

The tension in the house was almost unbearable. Jemma grumbled something unpleasant under her breath before she gathered her books and went upstairs.

"Tomorrow will be a big day," she mumbled. "Chemistry test, then boo hag hunting." For a fleeting moment, her mother's face came into her mind. "Never thought that was what my life would turn out to be without you, huh?"

She switched off the lamp like she switched off thoughts of her mother. She hoped Tad was doing the same thing.

Jemma went to bed, hoping for deep sleep and no disturbance from her supernatural stalker.

Jemma stood by the living room window, arms folded as she looked at the yard and the road where it dropped off. The sun had set behind the mountain, leaving the sky a hazy lilac burned at the edges by dark but radiant yellows. The shadows grew and thickened like arms reaching to grasp her. Was the boo hag waiting for the darkness? Jemma shuddered. It seemed likely.

She heard shifting from the kitchen and turned to see her father walk into the living room. His eyes lifted from the paper in his hand to meet hers. "You've been doing better in school."

Jemma nodded and turned back to the window. She heard Tad sigh. "I'll make dinner. After we eat, maybe we can rethink your work schedule. It'll be too cold for Mama B to be outside much. You'll need to help her prepare the grounds for the winter before the snow comes."

Jemma's heart thudded. *He has no idea what Mama B can handle,* she thought. She made no verbal response, just turned back to him and nodded. For this plan to work, she needed to play nice. *I hate this*, she thought. *I hate all this sneaking and lying, but I don't have any other choice.*

Tad sighed again. "We can't go on like this, Jem. All this silence around each other. It's not like us."

Jemma stiffened. "Well, it's like you said. I've changed."

Hurt flickered across Tad's face. He cleared his throat to respond but couldn't speak, so he retreated into the kitchen. Jemma regretted her words and tone but didn't know how she was supposed to repair the damage. *He kept secrets from me first. He broke his promise first.* Hardened in her resolve, Jemma followed him into the kitchen to see what he was making for dinner. She had her hand clenched around the glass bottle with the draught Easter had made in the pocket of her loose cargo pants.

"Iced tea tonight, Dad?" She tried to sound cheerful.

Tad mustered a smile. "That would be nice, Jem."

Jemma took the pitcher of iced tea from the refrigerator and poured him a glass. When his back was turned, she poured the draught into his drink. "Sugar?"

Still with his back turned, Tad replied, "Well, of course!"

Jemma stirred the tea as if she had just put sugar in as Tad turned to face her, his smile looking less forced. Jemma mustered a smile of her own, but it felt wrong. She fought off the feeling while her father made supper. She fought it off while he sat across from her at the table and began to eat. For a while, Jemma wondered if he knew what she was up to since he didn't touch his drink until his food was almost gone. Finally, he took a long gulp. Jemma watched as fatigue overtook him. He began to mumble incoherently, then his eyelids dipped shut, and his head bumped the table.

The journal pages hadn't indicated how long the sleeping draught would last, so Jemma called Val. "We have to move."

"We're coming. Be there in ten."

Jemma waited for them on the porch, hugging her coat tightly around her. The last of the light vanished from the sky. Darkness crept in, and with it, a piercing cold. The wind tore at the trees. The conditions were less than pleasant. Jemma gritted her teeth. *Push through it.* She had repeated these three words over and over in her training. This was different; the stakes were higher.

A minute later, Val's truck appeared and pulled into her driveway. Jemma's eyes widened when she saw both Easter and Mama B climb out. She had known Mama B would be coming, but it seemed strange to see her here since she hadn't left Gran's Rest in several years. Mama B looked around with narrowed eyes and nodded.

She knows this place. She remembers being here, Jemma realized, then remembered the former owner's picture had been in the photo album alongside Mama B's. The old witch carried a large leather pack. She glanced around the darkening yard. "Very good. Let's get to work."

Easter looked at Jemma with a worried expression. "What about your father?"

"He's asleep," Jemma answered. Neither mentioned the sleeping draught. Val and Mama B gave her confused looks, so Jemma passed it off with, "Gave him something to help him sleep." It wasn't a lie. She hoped they would assume Tad had been given medication.

The wind ripped at Jemma's hair and clothes. Easter

moved close to her to shield herself from the weather. "What now?" Val's voice cracked and quaked.

Mama B shuffled close to the door and bent to where Jemma had carved the warding sigil weeks ago. "It's fading," the old woman murmured. She looked at Jemma. "The boo hag has been able to get past some of the warding but not all of it. We want her to feel the wards come down. Then we will surround her. She'll be confused and not know who to attack."

"Then we'll attack *her*," Jemma added.

Mama B shook her head. "I will. You will watch me, Jemma."

Jemma glowered. *What is the point of all my training if I can't use what I've learned?* It didn't seem like a good moment to argue with Mama B, though, so she kept her mouth shut.

Val straightened, fists clenched at his sides. "I'm ready." He looked the opposite.

Easter's voice trembled. "Why don't we put the herbs the boo hag is attracted to on ourselves? It'll confuse her even more."

Mama B smiled approvingly. "You've been paying attention to my instructions, my dear. That is exactly what we must do." From her leather pouch, Mama B withdrew glass containers of the herbs she, Jemma, and Easter had gathered days ago. Jemma wrinkled her nose as she rubbed the odorous substance on her chest and arms.

"This better work because I'm going to need a long-ass shower after this," she muttered.

Easter and Val spread the herbs on their chests and arms without complaint. Jemma thought that if anyone was watching them now, they would think they were in a cult. All those rumors about her working for a witch would be proven true. Jemma put her head up. "Let's get this damn boo hag to come say hello."

They went to the back of the house. Mama B had gone there while they were spreading the herbs on their bodies. They found her standing in a trance. Her eyes were closed, and her hands were extended. Vague tendrils of blue light flowed from her fingers.

"What is she doing?" Val whispered.

"Opening the ward for the boo hag to come to us," Jemma answered. Mama B had made her practice this spell. It included speaking a string of words in a language Jemma didn't know under her breath while focusing her energy on the place in the ward she wanted to open.

Jemma's eyes widened. The longer Mama B worked, the more of the ward Jemma could see. It looked like a thin, shimmering veil suspended in midair. She could not see where it began or ended. She gasped. She could feel its trembling energy. It was heavy and warm and buzzing. A surge of energy passed over her skin.

Easter had a similar reaction. She reached for Jemma's hand and squeezed it. "Can you see it?"

Jemma nodded.

"See what?" Val demanded.

It seemed the veil could only be seen by the women. Jemma didn't take the time to answer him. Something was happening. Her instinct was to scream and run in the other direction, but the figure that stumbled out of the dark grove of trees beyond the ward kept her rooted to the spot.

The creature was so ugly she could not tear her eyes away as much as she wanted to.

The boo hag was as much shadow as flesh, a sack of bones with strings of bloody tissue hanging off her. Her eyes were white, devoid of pupils, and staring, and her head was cocked to the side. It wasn't as terrifying from a distance, but the image of the creature on Easter as she slept stole the breath from Jemma's lungs as it lunged forward, trying to jump through the opening in the ward.

The scent of the herbs made the boo hag salivate. Her mouth gaped to reveal a row of needle-like teeth covered in the same dripping tissue. Panic jolted through Jemma. It was the same feeling as having the monster beneath the bed grab her exposed leg or missing a step on a darkened stairwell. It felt like being sucked back by the shadows while running out of a pitch-black room after turning off the light.

Jemma wanted to run, but she gripped Easter's arm and stayed where she was. Mama B kept her stance, teeth gritted as the boo hag thrashed beyond the ward. The creature lifted its head like an animal on the hunt and sniffed.

She smells the herbs. She smells us. Jemma felt a thrumming within her, a warm buzz behind her heart in the deepest part of her being. *"The Art"* were the two words that came to mind. The thought didn't sound like her voice, though. It was a deeper, more distant, and far older voice she had never heard before. Jemma leaned into it. It came back, fainter this time but still there. *The Art is strong within you. Feel it. Use it.*

Jemma didn't know how to react to the voice. It didn't feel

threatening, and she sensed she didn't have a choice but to listen. The voice faded as Jemma heard something like a sob. It ripped her away from the crawling creature to the person from which the sound had come. Mama B strained against the black power leaking out of the creature opposite her. The boo hag snarled and extended its clawed hands, trying to snatch at Mama B's cloak, which trailed on the ground.

"No!" Jemma shrieked.

Easter tried to hold her back. "Jemma!"

Jemma tore out of her grip, bounded toward Mama B, and skidded to a halt a few feet in front of her. "Jemma, no!" came Mama B's hoarse voice.

Jemma was determined to see this through. The voice came into her mind again. *Her power is weakening. One or the other will have to be destroyed.* Jemma knew this task fell to only one witch, but she couldn't help herself. Pain contorted the old witch's face, and a strangled cry was wrenched from Mama B's throat.

Now! It was the voice again, that deep, ancient voice that did not belong to Jemma. The tone was urgent, almost threatening. The creature thrashed on the ground. *It's trapped!* Jemma realized. The only thing left was to bind and seal its power. That seemed almost too simple. Why was Mama B struggling so hard?

Teeth gritted and feet planted firmly on the ground, Jemma braced herself. The energy within her welled up, and she pushed her hands forth. Streams of light like those that had come from Mama B's hands flowed out. They were small and weak since she had never used them before. Her power flowed, getting stronger the longer her energy built up. She watched as it wrapped around the creature like vines choking it.

The boo hag's wails were cut off, and it raised its clawed hands to tear at the blue light around its throat. *It's weakening*, Jemma realized. Relief, however, was far from her reach. The next instant, the blue tendrils around the boo hag snapped like twigs and fell around the creature. The power from Jemma's hands faded, and her heart hammered. What the hell was happening? She could feel the boo hag's power rising and pressing against her. It was wild, unfocused, animalistic.

"No way in hell is this going to happen to me!" Jemma hissed. She braced herself again, and with a wild cry, made the declaration using the words Mama B had taught her. She still didn't know what they meant, but she could feel their meaning in her body. Blue light blasted from her hands, colliding with the boo hag and sending it reeling to the ground.

Panting, Mama B straightened. "Good!"

Jemma couldn't believe it. She had done it. She had bound the loathsome creature. The boo hag flailed on the ground, defeated. Its power was gone.

But it was not dead, Jemma realized. Fear filled her. Mama B had said the process would destroy one or the other, yet here they both were, still alive. That meant it wasn't over.

Jemma trembled even as the boo hag shriveled up. She became a dried husk, crumbling into black dust. The remains of the boo hag exploded. From where it had lain came a thick, dark gas. Jemma coughed and covered her nose and mouth. It was the worst thing she had ever smelled, reeking of corruption and buried secrets and old evil; evil from so long ago, it had laid in wait far longer than Jemma had been alive.

This wasn't supposed to happen! Looking at Mama B and seeing the dread filling her face, Jemma knew the older witch hadn't expected it either. "What now?" Jemma croaked, voice and face full of desperation. The dark presence welled up, and before Jemma could make another move or speak, it plunged toward her house.

A window shattered. The formless creature had launched itself into Jemma's house. "No!" she screamed, remembering that her father was asleep in the kitchen. She rushed toward him. Her heart pounded so fast it felt like it would tear itself from her chest.

Coughs and cries came from behind her. "Jem, don't go after it!" Mama B screamed. Easter was bent over on the ground, coughing up gas from her lungs as her brother attempted to help her.

Jemma plunged into the kitchen through the back door and stopped short, rooted to the spot with sudden dread and terror. The dark presence hovered over her father as if it were prepared to strike. This wasn't a boo hag. It was something new and far worse.

The next instant, Mama B appeared out of thin air. Her face was contorted with the same shock and fear Jemma wore. "Oh, child!" the old witch wailed. "You didn't tell me you used magic to put him to sleep!" The terror in her voice made Jemma realize she had done something very bad.

It was like time had stopped for a moment. She watched the creature hover, knowing it had made for her father because it had sensed the magic at work within him. Tad Nox was the most vulnerable, unprotected person the monster could go after, and Jemma was helpless to stand against it. Her body was too weak from binding the boo hag. The energy she had drawn on before had faded. The voice in the back of her mind had vanished.

Mama B wasn't finished, though. She braced herself, eyes blazing. "This isn't your house!" she shouted at the creature. "You don't belong here!" She shouted other words, an incantation Jemma had not yet learned containing words she did not know. She could feel them, though. Their power was incredible and made her want to run.

The dark presence hovering over her father didn't like it either, but the incantation didn't stop it from pressing closer. Jemma's eyes filled with tears, and she trembled as she watched Tad's body spasm. Though his eyes were still closed, his mouth opened, and he gibbered hateful, nonsensical things. The voice was not his own. It was deeper, darker, and colder.

"Help him!" Jemma screamed. *"Help him!"* The desperation in her body welled up until it could not be contained. As if it had heard her words, the creature wrenched its form toward Jemma, still holding onto her father, black tendrils of power wrapped around his neck. The words spewing from his mouth were choked off.

"Hold onto me, child!" Mama B shouted. Jemma couldn't move, but she had to. She had to hold onto the witch to be protected. Jemma didn't remember moving. All she knew was that a second later, her hands clutched the back of Mama B's cloak. Wind coursed through the house.

It must have come from the witch because Jemma couldn't see any other sign of her power. The blue tendrils of light did not emerge from her hands.

Mama B shrieked one last word, and the creature lost its grip on the sleeping man at the table. It flailed as well as a formless blob of darkness could, emitting a deep, warbling wail. Then, with a declaration of pure power, Mama B blasted the creature back. Another window broke, but Jemma didn't care. Her father slumped, breathing evenly again but still asleep.

She rushed forward. Tad's face was covered in sweat. His skin was too pale. Crying, she begged, "Please help him!" Sounds at the back door reached Jemma's ears. A second later, Easter and Val stumbled into the kitchen, eyes wide with terror.

"Is it gone?" Val stammered.

"It's gone," Easter murmured as she clutched her brother's arm.

Mama B placed a warm, comforting hand on Jemma's shoulder. "Your father is going to be fine."

Jemma looked at the witch. "You saved him." A tear slipped down her cheek.

Mama B's eyes also welled up. "I couldn't have if you hadn't bound and sealed the boo hag's power."

Jemma stood up on shaking legs, realizing that none of them knew what had possessed the boo hag. The creature was gone, and the boo hag was black dust in the grass, but they had more questions now than they had had before.

Mama B pulled something out of her leather pack. "I don't know about the three of you, but after all that, I'm starving." Jemma spied a loaf of bread and a jar of preserves in her hands. Her eyes flitted to the table as her father stirred. His eyes opened, but it took him a moment to realize who stood in front of him. Confusion creased his brow.

"I think I just had the most awful nightmare," he murmured in a dazed voice.

Shaking and smiling with relief, Jemma threw her arms around him. "Mama B brought us something to eat, Dad."

CHAPTER TWENTY-TWO

There were conversations to be held and dozens of questions to ask and find answers to, but Mama B waved away any words from Jemma, Val, Easter, and a disoriented Tad. He was wondering why four people, including three teenagers and an old woman, were in his house in the middle of the night. "First, we rest. We will talk tomorrow," Mama B commanded, more to Tad than to the teenagers.

Easter and Val phoned their parents to tell them they were spending the night. Easter sank onto the sofa, still looking dazed but sighing with relief. "It's good to know I'll never have to deal with a boo hag sucking the breath out of me while I sleep again."

Jemma smiled with relief as well, but she wasn't as sure. The dark presence had been driven away but not defeated. She shivered at the thought of its return. After she set up sleeping arrangements for Easter and Val and Mama B in the living room, Jemma attended to her father. "I need you to explain what happened to me right now," he pressed. His voice was weak.

"In the morning, Tad. Right now, we all need to go to bed." She paused, knowing her lack of explanation would mean he'd be up all night worrying. "You got sick after dinner and fell asleep, so I called Mama B to help." Tad didn't seem satisfied, but it also didn't seem like he knew Jemma was lying. At last, he submitted and went to bed.

"Now I need a shower," Jemma muttered. She was so tired after getting clean that when she climbed into bed, her fatigue overtook the swarm of questions swirling in her mind. "Tomorrow," she whispered as she fell asleep.

Jemma awoke with a start. She did not know what had awakened her, but she was relieved to find her room was not dark. Early morning sunlight filtered in through the blinds in the loft. She started as she turned her head and found she was not alone. Mama B sat in a chair beside her bed, smiling down at her. "How long have you been there?" Jemma hissed groggily as she sat up.

Mama B chuckled, but then her amusement faded. She reached for Jemma's hand. "I want to speak to you first, child." Her expression turned firm. Jemma knew she was about to be reprimanded. "If there's been anything you were supposed to learn, it was that you are to never engage in the Art without my help until you are strong and knowledgeable on your own!" Mama B whispered so she would not awaken those sleeping below, but her rebuke was still effective.

Jemma stared at the blankets on her bed, unable to look the old witch in the eyes. Mama B sighed. "I understand why you did it, though." Jemma lifted her head to find Mama B wearing a tired smile. She looked as though she hadn't slept a wink. "You are resourceful, Jemma Nox, and brave. Sometimes the two are deadly when you don't think about the consequences. Magic doesn't solve problems. It just moves those problems to a different place."

Jemma remembered that concept being introduced in her training. This idea was that the law of conservation of energy was the same for magic and trouble. Magic couldn't wipe away trouble, only move it into a different form. *And that was exactly what happened when I bound the boo hag but whatever was inside of it came out,* Jemma guessed.

"The new form might be easier to handle than the original," Mama B continued, "but magic isn't about whipping together a potion that will cure all ills." She gave Jemma an earnest look. "Life is hard no matter what. You know that by now."

Jemma nodded. A lump formed in her throat.

Mama B squeezed her hand. "Magic lets you pick your hard."

So far, it seemed Jemma had picked the wrong hard. "But it's all working out, isn't it?"

Mama B did not answer right away. Then, sighing, she replied, "I hope so, my dear, but I cannot be certain." She paused again, her eyes going to the closet in Jemma's room. Her gaze halted there, and recognition crossed her face. She did not speak, though, so whatever thoughts came into her mind were not revealed to Jemma. "I do not know what that dark presence was." Her eyes met Jemma's.

Jemma's heart pounded. "Do you think it will come back?"

Mama B shrugged. "Hard to say. Whatever it was, it was older and far more evil than the boo hag. It had latched onto the weakened creature, and it was as bad for the boo hag as the boo hag was for Easter."

Jemma gulped. "Do you think that thing was the reason the boo hag acted abnormally?"

Mama B nodded. "We have one question answered and more presented." Concern deepened the wrinkles on her face. "Something like that only comes from places of deep corruption and evil." She shook her head in disbelief. "I did not think such places existed so close to Kalhoun County, but it seems I was wrong. I have been a recluse for too long, and events may have gotten away from me."

Jemma's brow creased. She didn't know what Mama B meant. The boo hag was gone, but the issue of what the dark presence was meant more struggle and danger lay ahead. Jemma drew a deep breath and thought about the voice she had heard the night before. She wanted to tell Mama B, but her head hurt too much. There were other things to deal with first.

"Are you ready to take on whatever comes next, my dear?" Mama B asked.

Jemma wasn't sure. She hesitated but then remembered she hadn't been ready for her mother to leave. She hadn't been prepared for her father's depression and their need to move. She hadn't been ready for a new life, but here she was, carrying it as if she had been born to do so.

She nodded, her resolve forming. "If I'm not ready now, I'll do whatever I need to become ready."

Mama B beamed. "That's my girl."

Warmth flowed through Jemma. She had missed the

feeling of family for the past several years since none of her mother's side of the family spoke to her or Tad anymore. Mama B felt like the family she was supposed to have—a doting grandmother and a fierce, wise mentor.

Mama B stood. "After your friends go home, we will speak with your father. I am sure he will need answers too."

Jemma deflated, but she nodded in agreement. Tad Nox deserved to know the whole truth. She was done keeping things from him.

She didn't want to lie and sneak anymore.

Tad Nox slept half the day, but Jemma wasn't angry. It gave her time to survey the broken windows and figure out how to fix them. Without the boo hag following her around, she was free to go into town to buy the supplies. "I'll be back in an hour or so," she told Mama B around midmorning. The old witch told her not to worry and that she would inform Tad of his daughter's whereabouts should he awaken before her return.

When Jemma returned, she found Mama B and her father sitting in the living room. Tad appeared much revived. Though he was still pale and looked like he needed another few hours of sleep, Mama B had made him a cup of the tea she often gave Jemma. The liquid soothed Tad and made him more comfortable with the witch's presence. He was even smiling while the two of them conversed as if they were old, well-acquainted friends. Jemma's heart warmed. Tad Nox had that effect on everyone. It was the reason her mother had fallen in love with him so many years ago and why she still thought he was the best dad on earth despite their occasional differences.

Jemma stopped on the threshold of the living room. "Come in, dear, and drink some tea with us," Mama B prompted. "It is high time the three of us had a good long talk." Jemma did as she was told, though she was afraid to look her father in the eye. His face was full of worry.

Where to start? Jemma wondered. Tell him the windows were broken by an angry magic blob of evil? Tell him my employer is the witch everyone says she is? Tell him I've been learning the abilities she has for weeks? Tell him a supernatural creature has been stalking us at night for over a month? Her mind buzzed. Mama B handed her the cup of tea, and Jemma's head cleared as she drank.

Mama B spoke first. "I suppose it would be best to start at the beginning." She turned to Jemma. "Tell your father about the journal you found and the brew you decided to make for Easter."

Jemma decided the best way to tell the story was from beginning to end, disclosing all details and answering all questions honestly. Tad remained quiet throughout the entire story without asking a single question. He knew when Jemma was being honest. She began by telling him how she had found the journal and the photo album and how hiding the box of mementos had been the first thing she'd done that changed their relationship. Then she hid the journal from him, and everything proceeded from there.

Tad's eyes widened as she spoke. He looked at Mama B

now and then for confirmation. Mama B nodded but did not interrupt Jemma.

"I know it all sounds batshit-crazy, Dad," Jemma said at the end of her story, "but I swear it's all true. Easter and Val will back me up. If you had seen what happened at that party, you'd be certain too."

Before Tad could respond, Mama B added, "It was my fault there was a strain on your relationship with your daughter and she fell behind on her schoolwork. I've been training her to properly defend herself against these new enemies. She is a teenage girl, yes, but she has been opened to a new world to explore beyond her physical surroundings."

Mama B peered earnestly at Tad Nox. "Years ago, I trained girls your daughter's age in the Art so they could carry on the tradition of the holler witches after I died. I wanted to train them to heal and help those around them. It was less about fighting off evil spirits back then, but things have changed. There is a darkness in these mountains that must be fought."

Mama B's language was interesting. Her tone changed depending on the complexity of her words. The southern twang drifted from her voice, replaced with more refined words. The Eloise Brickellwood who'd once lived elsewhere emerged but was eventually rejoined by the kind old woman Jemma had come to know.

"After everything that happened and ending up alone on the mountain," Mama B continued, "I vowed that the next young woman who came to me showing promise would become my apprentice."

Tad chuckled, which surprised the old woman and his

daughter. "I suppose it is my fault this started, then." He pushed his round glasses up his nose. "It was my idea for Jemma to work for you." He looked at his daughter, eyes glowing with pride. "I am glad she did since you have become a wonderful friend and mentor to her. And I'm sorry for breaking my promise to you, Jemma. If I hadn't, you wouldn't have felt the need to hide things from me."

Jemma couldn't believe what she was hearing. She had expected her father to be in complete denial about their experiences, but it seemed he had no choice but to believe them. Further, he apologized for everything she needed him to apologize for.

"Jemma isn't the only one who shows potential in the Art," Mama B remarked. "Easter McCarthy shows much promise as well. I think that eventually, the group of girls I once taught could be rebuilt." She winked at Jemma. "We'll be a force to be reckoned with." She cleared her throat and lifted her chin a little higher. "That, along with the fact that I've been alone for far too long, is why I have decided to reopen Gran's Rest in time for the holidays."

Jemma and Tad exchanged looks of delight. Mama B looked at Jemma, smiling broadly. "I would be more than happy to have Jemma Nox as my head groundskeeper, and if her friends the McCarthys would like to join my staff as well, they are more than welcome. Of course, much more recruiting will need to be done. I'll need a cook and cleaners and…well, I'll figure all that out." She waved a dismissive hand. "I've handled far more difficult things in my life."

Jemma knew the woman sitting before her was a wellspring of stories, and she hoped to be friends with her long enough to hear them all. She sat beside her father and put an arm around his neck. "And we'll help! Tad can't wait to have a list of things to fix. You know he's been pretty excited about fixing things up around here."

Tad chuckled. "Starting with the two broken windows in the kitchen."

Mama B directed her attention to Tad. "I am aware that your daughter was sentenced to house arrest until her grades are back up, and I will insist upon her schoolwork being finished before she comes to work each day if you will allow it. I can't do this without her."

Tad shook the old woman's hand, grinning. "I think we've got a deal."

Mama B sat back and observed father and daughter. "You know, Gran's Rest has always been a place of healing. I think it would do you both some good to spend more time up there." She didn't state what kind of healing they would need, but she seemed to read their life story as if it was written before her. Perhaps, with enough time at Gran's Rest, Jemma could put her mother and her life in Hendricks behind her for good. The box of mementos she had taken wouldn't matter anymore. At least, that was what she hoped.

Tad's eyes moved from Mama B to Jemma. He nodded after a moment of reflection, then, drawing Jemma into a hug, said, "We both have some healing to do. I am glad to be given a place where we can do that."

Jemma had to hold back tears as memories both good and bad flooded into her mind.

When she pulled away, Tad asked, "How do you plan to

advertise for the Gran's Rest grand reopening? Do you have any experience with online marketing?"

Mama B frowned. "Don't you see how old I am?" Her question dared him to make a humorous remark. She laughed at his hesitancy. "I know much about magic and herbs, but I'd warrant those little screens were designed by the devil."

"Or just people," Jemma added.

Mama B chuckled, wagged a finger, and addressed Tad. "Your daughter is wise beyond her years. You'd better pay attention to anything she says."

Jemma smiled.

Mama B rose to her feet. "We have a lot of work to do. It's going to be cold soon. Today, I think we're going to chop firewood."

CHAPTER TWENTY-THREE

Jemma Nox was now employed as the groundskeeper of Gran's Rest, the bed and breakfast on the mountain that was soon to have its grand reopening. That meant Jemma was the subject of much speculation—even more than she already was. Many strange things had occurred in Kalhoun County over the years, but a teenage girl in charge of an estate's grounds was not one of them.

"A teenage girl in charge of the grounds? I've never heard of such a thing! That old lady Mrs. Brickellwood is losing her mind. She's been losing it for quite some time," some said.

The idea of a bed and breakfast opening as the first snow came to Kalhoun County had many of the locals perplexed. Eloise Brickellwood hadn't been seen in town for years, and now she was opening her place of business again? It was Jemma's opinion that the growing speculation was a good thing. The more questions people asked, the more curiosity would build, and more people would make their way up the mountain to see for themselves what was going on.

"Get them talking in whatever way we can," Tad had instructed Easter, Val, and Jemma. The McCarthys had taken flyers to school and passed them to people they knew and those they didn't.

When the people who were curious about Mrs. Brickellwood reached Gran's Rest, they would find tamed and beautiful grounds, a glowing house with warm hearths, cozy bedrooms for guests to stay the night, a stable with two new horses, and a kind old woman who made the best marmalade in the area.

The rumors would eventually fade, kept alive only by those who were too narrow-minded to accept Mrs. Brickellwood. Jemma thought about the town elders in Mama B's stories and decided she wasn't going to put up with any such person.

As the new groundskeeper, Jemma received strange looks whenever she went into Solomon's Cross. She went on her way, ignoring them or smiling to herself. *They'll have to come up the mountain to see my work!*

Groundskeeping didn't only entail making sure the gardens looked good. She spent her days procuring herbs and plants when the weather was good and inside, sorting and experimenting under Mama B's supervision when it was cold.

Jemma had decided that after everything she had been through so far, caring about what people thought was a waste of time. Everything wasn't how it seemed, including Kalhoun County. "I have a feeling I've only touched the surface of what is to be discovered in Kalhoun County and

Solomon's Cross," Jemma told Easter the day before the grand reopening when she went into town for supplies.

"I've lived here all my life, and I feel the same way," Easter replied with a sigh. "I've been too sick for too long to care about anything else." She smiled, and Jemma noticed how well her friend looked. Easter's hair was growing back at a rapid pace. Her dark eyes shimmered with enthusiasm whenever they were at Gran's Rest. Color had returned to her complexion. She walked straighter and with more confidence. The confidence, Jemma knew, hadn't just come from feeling better. Mama B had taken her friend under her wing and given her tasks in preparation for the opening.

Jemma made her way into town, with Tad driving her. "You know, Jem, I'm surprised by how much attention is on Gran's Rest," he mentioned.

"Why do you say that?"

"Well, it's this," Tad started as he took his truck around a sharp bend in the mountain road. "She's had all kinds of nasty rumors surrounding her for years. It's a wonder anyone would want to stay the night at her place of business. But then again, I think all the rumors have drawn curiosity. People are coming here because they have to find out if what they've heard is true."

Jemma nodded and smiled. "It's good news for Solomon's Cross, don't you think? Tourists and all. It could help the people here a lot."

Tad nodded, but he did not smile. "I've heard some mutterings in town. Not everyone is happy about it."

Jemma frowned. "Well, they're going to have to deal with it. Besides, Easter and Val have been recruiting in other towns nearby. They aren't bothering the people here about switching jobs." Finding employees for Gran's Rest had been difficult at first, but an influx of curious minds from a couple of towns over had staffed Gran's Rest before the big day. Jemma could even have help on the grounds if she wanted it, though it wouldn't matter until the spring.

Mama B had given father and daughter a lengthy list, so they decided to split it up and meet when they were finished. A soft sheet of snow settled on the sidewalk and the street in the main part of town. Jemma normally hated the cold, but she didn't mind it now. It only seemed right for it to snow in the mountains, and she was beginning to feel at home here at last. Thanksgiving was coming, and following it was a month of holiday cheer. In the past few years, Jemma had spent Thanksgiving stuck between lost seasons of happiness and an unknown future. This year would be different. She was determined that would be so.

"Why don't we race to see who's done first, Jemma?" Tad asked as he parked in town. His eyes sparkled.

Jemma grinned. "I'm going to win, though. You can't go anywhere without talking to every single person you meet."

Tad winked. "That's what you think." He got out of the truck and sprinted toward the store he needed to go into first. Rolling her eyes and laughing, Jemma climbed out of the passenger side. Snow crunched under her feet. A voice from behind her diverted her attention.

"Jemma?" the person asked, then more excitedly, "Jemma, it *is* you!"

Jemma didn't recognize the voice, but when she turned, she saw Jade bounding toward her. She had forgotten how tall the other girl was. Jade also didn't have a purple streak in her hair anymore. That wasn't the only thing that was different about her. She looked tired. Bags hung under her eyes. She wasn't wearing her winged eyeliner like she usually did. Jemma stiffened and turned away, hoping Jade would think she hadn't heard her.

"Come on, Jemma. I just want to talk to you," the other girl pleaded.

Jemma turned, not hiding the reluctance on her face. "Look," Jade started as she dragged a hand through her dark hair, "I wanted to tell you I'm sorry about what I said about Easter. Cameron and I were talking, and we wanted to get something for her." Jade had had her arm behind her back this whole time but moved it to show a bouquet of pink roses. "Will you give these to her and this card?" She handed Jemma a "get well soon" card.

Jemma's eyes widened, and she mustered a smile. "I will give it to her. And no worries. All is forgiven."

"Good, good." Jade looked relieved. "I've heard Easter is doing a lot better. Her illness is going away, isn't it?" Jemma nodded, and Jade continued. "When Val told us you hated his sister, we thought he was making shit up and that you needed friends. I was trying to help." Jade shrugged, and Jemma's mouth fell open.

"Val told you that? When?"

Jade shrugged again. "A week before the party, maybe? Something like that. That was why I was surprised when he brought you. I thought he wanted nothing to do with you."

Stunned, Jemma tried to sort through her thoughts. Was Jade lying, or had Val been trying to keep Jemma away from his sister? It was possible, Jemma thought, since he was so against her getting medicine from Mama B for Easter in the beginning. She could only hope that he had changed his mind about her and the old witch.

Jemma tried not to let the revelation bother her, especially in front of Jade. She pulled a flyer from the inside of her jacket and handed it to the girl. "Gran's Rest will be reopening soon." She smiled. "If you or anyone you know would like to book a nice, cozy place for the holidays, let us know."

Jade tapped the photograph on the front of the flyer. "Easter took these, didn't she?"

Jemma nodded. "How did you know?"

Jade's eyes shone. "She used to love photography but gave it up when she got sick. I'm glad she's doing something she loves again."

Jemma smiled. "Yeah, me too."

Jade thanked Jemma and made her way down the street. Jemma stood in the falling snow, feeling warm inside. *I'll think about Val later*, she decided as she made her way across the street to RJ's hardware store.

Jemma hadn't been inside the store since the first time and entered with dread twisting her stomach into knots. One of the last people she wanted to see was AJ Kilmer. The first person she saw, however, was not the younger Kilmer but the older. RJ gave her a broad smile. "Jemma Nox, isn't it? I remember you and your father."

Jemma smiled back. "Yes, I remember you too."

"How are you and your old man doin'? Getting' settled in all right?"

"All right" was relative, but she nodded. "How's AJ?" She

hadn't decided she would ask. The words just popped out of her mouth. Sometimes, the automatic politeness taught to her by her father worked ahead of her brain.

RJ's smile faded into a crumbling look of sadness. "Well, he'll be out of the way for a little while, that's for sure. Afterwards, he'll serve two months' probation."

Jemma's brows furrowed. "I thought Mama B wasn't going to press charges for the break-in?"

RJ shook his head. "He wasn't charged for that. Other recent offenses."

Jemma didn't know what to say. She knew some of AJ's acting out had been beyond his control. She mustered a smile. "I'm sure everything will get better, Mr. Kilmer." With the boo hag gone, it wouldn't be following AJ around. RJ didn't have this same assurance, but he seemed comforted by Jemma's words regardless.

"I thank ya for sayin' that." He bobbed his head in gratitude.

Jemma pulled a second flyer from her coat pocket. "If any of your daughters are planning to come to Kalhoun County for the holidays, they are welcome to stay at Gran's Rest. It opens this weekend."

RJ glanced at the flyer. Whatever thoughts he might have had about Mama B and the mountain, he didn't make them known to Jemma. He continued to speak to her cheerfully. "Well, thank ya for givin' me this. We'll just have to see 'bout that. Now, what is it you came in here to get, young lady?"

The wind was cold, and snow lay on the ground, but Jemma Nox felt warm inside. She stood between her smiling father and a beaming Eloise Brickellwood. The old witch would spend the next several days telling her guests, "No, it's Mama B. Don't be calling me anything but that."

On the other side of Mama B stood Easter, and next to her was Val. Jemma hadn't had a chance to confront him, but she was fine with waiting. She wanted to revel in the glow of what she had helped Mama B produce these past few months.

I came to this town wanting a new life, she thought. Chuckling to herself, she added, *I'm the groundskeeper for Gran's Rest. Who would have thought? And a witch on top of that?*

Around them stood the new staff of Gran's Rest. Some of them were young like Jemma, but others were older like her father. All had come because they had curious minds and tender souls. The first day of interviews had ended with Mama B hiring every single person who came calling. "Many wounds to be healed here," she had told Jemma.

This place was more than a bed and breakfast. Jemma had come to realize that before it was open. This was a restoration of a piece of history, and it was bringing back something that was desperately needed in the world. *This isn't just a place of rest*, Jemma thought. *It's for treatment and recovery. We're all going to heal here, and in ways that aren't only physical.*

She shifted as a note of fear crept into her thoughts. Setting out to heal meant creating a light that would make them a target since light would draw in unfriendly things. *I'd rather have those things exposed in the light instead of letting them creep around in the dark, snatching the vulnerable, the ignorant, and the innocent,* Jemma thought. Faces filled her mind: AJ Kilmer first, and her mother, Delilah Nox last. Perhaps her mother had left her because she was lost.

Jemma's eyes scanned the grounds as the first car came up the slope. This place was healing her. It was giving her the space to forgive, even though the person she needed to forgive wasn't around.

A warm, comforting hand came to rest on Jemma's shoulder. She looked into Mama B's face. The old woman was excited and a little nervous. As she should be, Jemma thought with a smile. She squeezed Mama B's hand. The older woman leaned close and whispered, "Thank you for all your help, my dear. None of this would have been possible without you."

She added. "I thought I'd be the last witch of Kalhoun County. I'm beginning to think maybe I won't be after all."

AUTHOR NOTES - MICHAEL ANDERLE

APRIL 21, 2022

Thank you for not only reading this book but these author notes as well. Without you supporting us (by reading our books either through Kindle Unlimited or purchasing them) we would not have the privilege of writing more stories!

Another Genre...sort of.

So, this book is a little more Cozy Urban Fantasy than Cozy or Urban Fantasy.

How so? Well, generally cozy mystery is older ladies who solve murders in their quaint town with no travel.

Urban Fantasy is often younger females with action, adventure, and tons and tons of magic.

This is a mix. *I hope you liked it!*

YA and me.

I have a habit of cursing. YA stories generally don't have much cursing, so it requires a team to pull out the worst of my mistakes in stories that lean (or could lean) toward a young-ish market

I think everyone who has read my books or knows me knows my predilection for adult word usage. Therefore, they know I can't and/or shouldn't write children's books.

I tried.

However, I figure little Tommy shouldn't use 'f#ck' in a sentence at two years old. There is a children's book series that has cursing, but even I draw the line somewhere. Cursing is something for young adults to try. Not toddlers.

(Editor's note: I once saw a boy of about four smoking in Sumatra. He was under a sign encouraging children not to smoke. I drew my line right there.)

Welcome...

So, welcome to a series with a bit of cozy, a bit of urban fantasy, and a bit of cursing. When someone asks, "Does that author curse in his stories?" pull down your glasses, look over the top, and say, 'It's an Anderle creation...of course he does. The question is merely, "What did the editors take out when Michael wasn't looking?"

(Editor's note: nothing. Dialogue seemed pretty authentic to me! Anyone who thinks young adults don't curse hasn't been listening.)

I hope you have a great week or weekend. I look forward to chatting with you in the next book.

Ad Aeternitatem,

Michael

Ok, now a little about me if you haven't met me.

I wrote my first book *Death Becomes Her* (*The Kurtherian*

Gambit) in September/October of 2015 and released it November 2, 2015. I wrote and released the next two books that same month and had three released by the end of November 2015.

So, just over six years ago.

Since then, I've written, collaborated, concepted, and/or created hundreds more in all sorts of genres.

My most successful genre is still my first, Paranormal Sci-Fi, followed quickly by Urban Fantasy. I have multiple pen names I produce under.

Some because I can be a bit crude in my humor at times or raw in my cynicism (Michael Todd). I have one I share with Martha Carr (Judith Berens, and another (not disclosed) that we use as a marketing test pen name.

In general, I just love to tell stories, and with success comes the opportunity to mix two things I love in my life.

Business and stories.

I've wanted to be an entrepreneur since I was a teenager. I was a very *unsuccessful* entrepreneur (I tried many times) until my publishing company LMBPN signed one author in 2015.

Me.

I was the president of the company, and I was the first author published. Funny how it worked out that way.

It was late 2016 before we had additional authors join me for publishing. Now we have a few dozen authors, a few hundred audiobooks by LMBPN published, a few hundred more licensed by six audio companies, and about a thousand titles in our company.

It's been a busy six plus years.

BOOKS BY MICHAEL ANDERLE

Sign up for the LMBPN email list to be notified of new releases and special deals!

https://lmbpn.com/email/

For a complete list of books by Michael Anderle, please visit:

www.lmbpn.com/ma-books/

CONNECT WITH THE AUTHORS

Michael Anderle Social

Website: http://lmbpn.com

Email List: http://lmbpn.com/email/

https://www.facebook.com/LMBPNPublishing

https://twitter.com/MichaelAnderle

https://www.instagram.com/lmbpn_publishing/

https://www.bookbub.com/authors/michael-anderle

www.ingramcontent.com/pod-product-compliance
Lightning Source LLC
LaVergne TN
LVHW041758060526
838201LV00046B/1038